THE WORLD'S CLASSICS

THE SHADOW-LINE

JOSEPH CONRAD was born Jósef Teodor Konrad Korzeniowski in the Russian part of Poland in 1857. His parents were punished by the Russians for their Polish nationalist activities and both died while Conrad was still a child. In 1874 he left Poland for France and in 1878 began a career with the British merchant navy. He spent nearly twenty years as a sailor and did not begin writing novels until he was approaching forty. He became a British citizen in 1886 and settled permanently in England after his marriage to Jessie George in 1896.

Conrad is a writer of extreme subtlety and sophistication; works such as *Heart of Darkness, Lord Jim* and *Nostromo* display technical complexities which have established Conrad as one of the first English 'Modernists'. He is also noted for the unprecedented vividness with which he communicates a pessimist's view of man's personal and social destiny in such works as *The Secret Agent, Under Western Eyes* and *Victory.* Despite the immediate critical recognition that they received in his life-time Conrad's major novels did not sell, and he lived in relative poverty until the commercial success of *Chance* (1913) secured for him a wider public and an assured income. In 1923 he visited America, with great acclaim, and he was offered a knighthood (which he declined) shortly before his death in 1924. Since then his reputation has steadily grown and he is now seen as a writer who revolutionized the English novel and was arguably the most important single innovator of the twentieth century.

JEREMY HAWTHORN was born in 1942 and is Professor of Modern British Literature at the University of Trondheim, Norway. He is the author of *Joseph Conrad: Language and Fictional Self-Consciousness.*

THE WORLD'S CLASSICS

JOSEPH CONRAD

The Shadow-Line

A Confession

'Worthy of my undying regard'

Edited with an Introduction by
JEREMY HAWTHORN

Oxford   New York
OXFORD UNIVERSITY PRESS

OX2 6DP

chi
okyo

and associated companies in
Beirut Berlin Ibadan Nicosia

Oxford is a trade mark of Oxford University Press

Introduction, Note on the Text, and Notes © Jeremy Hawthorn 1985
Bibliography and Chronology © John Batchelor 1983

This edition first published as a World's Classics paperback 1985
Reprinted 1986, 1987

British Library Cataloguing in Publication Data
Conrad, Joseph
The shadow-line: a confession.—(The
World's classics)
I. Title
823'.912 [F]   PR6005.04
ISBN 0–19–281686–1

Library of Congress Cataloging in Publication Data
Conrad, Joseph, 1857–1924.
The shadow-line.
(The World's classics)
Bibliography: p.
I. Title.
PR6005 04S5   1985   823'.912   84 25401
ISBN 0–19–281686–1 (pbk.)

Printed in Great Britain by
Hazell Watson & Viney Limited
Aylesbury, Bucks

CONTENTS

INTRODUCTION

The ship, this ship, our ship, the ship we serve, is the moral symbol of our life.[1]

JOSEPH CONRAD wrote these words in 1918, two years after the publication of *The Shadow-Line*, but they express a belief that is exemplified in everything he wrote concerning ships and the sea. *The Shadow-Line* is one of a group of Conrad's works—written at different times in his life—which draw on his experiences during his third trip to the East in 1887-8.[2] Conrad had sailed from Amsterdam to Java, but was injured by a falling spar during the trip and ended up spending six weeks in hospital in Singapore. Afterwards, he signed on as mate of the *Vidar*, which traded among the islands of the Malayan archipelago, signing off four and a half months later, just as the narrator of *The Shadow-Line* signs off his ship at the start of the story. He was offered his one and only command on a seagoing vessel shortly after this, and travelled from Singapore to Bangkok on the *Melita* to take over as captain of the *Otago*, an iron barque or sailing ship. After a short stay in Bangkok he sailed to Sydney, calling in at Singapore to replenish his supply of medicine.

This relatively brief period provided Conrad with experiences which appear, in different forms and with different emphases, in *Lord Jim* (1900), *The End of the Tether* (1902), *Falk* (1903), *The Secret Sharer* (1910), *A Smile of Fortune* (1911), and *The Shadow-Line* (1916). They are also referred to in the non-fictional *The Mirror of the Sea* (1906).

On a number of occasions Conrad used the word 'autobiography' in connection with *The Shadow-Line*, and clearly its basic

---

[1] Joseph Conrad, 'Well Done' (1918), in *Notes on Life and Letters* (Dent Collected Edition, reprinted London, 1970), p. 188.

[2] For the information that follows I am heavily indebted to Norman Sherry, *Conrad's Eastern World* (Cambridge, Cambridge University Press, 1966).

plot corresponds quite closely to Conrad's own experiences. Moreover the names of many of the characters in the tale are close to, or identical with, many real people with whom Conrad came into contact during 1887–8.[3] Captain Ellis *was* Master-Attendant at Singapore (Conrad had used the name Eliott in *Lord Jim* and *The End of the Tether*, and in his manuscript of *The Shadow-Line* he starts to use the same name, changing it on second thoughts—perhaps because the real Ellis was now dead—back to Ellis). There *was* a John Niven who was engineer on the *Vidar*, and Conrad's first mate on the *Otago* was a Mr Born, who appears as Mr Burns in a number of Conrad's books apart from *The Shadow-Line*. In *The End of the Tether* Captain Eliott refers to a certain Hamilton whom he describes as 'the worst loafer of them all', and whom he forces to accept a command he does not want.

The difference between this last detail and the account of the way in which Conrad's narrator in *The Shadow-Line* obtains his command despite the Steward's attempt to give it to Hamilton should alert us to the fact that in none of these stories can we assume that we are dealing with 'exact autobiography'[4], as Conrad inadvisedly described *The Shadow-Line*. About *A Smile of Fortune* and *The Secret Sharer* in his 'Author's Note' to *'Twixt Land and Sea*, Conrad wrote that notwithstanding their autobiographical form they were not 'the record of personal

---

[3] I have again relied heavily on Sherry here.

[4] Norman Sherry refers to two letters written by Conrad in 1917, to his agent J. B. Pinker and to his friend Sidney Colvin. Both letters refer to *The Shadow-Line* as autobiographical, and the identical term 'exact autobiography' appears in each letter (see Sherry, p. 211). Frederick Karl refers to a letter from Conrad to John Quinn written in 1915 in which Conrad uses the phrase 'a sort of autobiography', and also to the letter to Colvin, in which Conrad gives the information that 'Giles is a Capt. Patterson, a very well known person there'. (See Frederick J. Karl, *Joseph Conrad: The Three Lives* (New York, Farrar, Straus and Giroux, 1979), pp. 773 and 779.) Gary Geddes quotes perhaps the most helpful of Conrad's comments from a letter to Helen Sanderson written after publication of the tale and included in G. Jean Aubry's *Joseph Conrad: Life and Letters*: '[it is a] piece of as strict autobiography as the form allowed,—I mean, the need of slight dramatization to make the thing actual. Very slight. For tne rest, not a fact or sensation is "invented"'. See Gary Geddes, *Conrad's Later Novels* (Montreal, McGill-Queen's University Press, 1980), p. 104.

experience', and this distinction may be usefully borne in mind with regard to *The Shadow-Line*. It is clear that *some* personal experience enters into this work, but Conrad has transformed not only certain external facts of the first voyage of the *Otago* under his command, but also some of his personal experiences during that trip.[5]

It is striking how different the tone of *The Shadow-Line* is from that of many of the previous stories which used the same set of experiences. There is little doubt that a major factor here is the date of *The Shadow-Line*'s composition. Although the story was first published in 1916–17, and was written in 1915, Conrad's earliest recorded reference to it (as *First Command*) comes in a letter written on 14 February 1899 to his publisher William Blackwood, concerning the stories he has planned, which include *A Seaman* (perhaps *Typhoon*) and *First Command*:

These are not written. They creep about in my head but [have] got to be caught and tortured into some kind of shape. I think—I think they would turn out good as good as (they say) *Youth* is.[6]

The 'torturing' took him almost sixteen years, and it is tempting to speculate whether this was because of the pressure of other work or a result of some less material problem—some psychological block. Such conjecture is necessarily inconclusive, but had *The Shadow-Line* been written in 1900, it is certain that it would have been a very different work.

In September 1915 Conrad's older son Borys had enlisted and become a second lieutenant, and although Conrad had been writing *The Shadow-Line* since the beginning of the year, he had certainly been conscious of the war even if its threat to his own immediate family only became clear a few months before he completed the manuscript. Frederick Karl quotes the

[5] For example, according to Sherry, by no means all of the crew of the *Otago* went down with malaria; John Snadden, the previous captain of the *Otago*, was apparently on good terms with Mr Born (Burns), was neither mad nor a bad captain, and did not even throw his violin (which he did possess) overboard!

[6] William Blackburn (ed.), *Joseph Conrad: Letters to William Blackwood and David S. Meldrum* (Durham, North Carolina, Duke University Press, 1958), p. 54.

comment Conrad himself wrote in Richard Curle's copy of the novel:

This story had been in my mind for some years. Originally I used to think of it under the name of *First Command*. When I managed in the second year of war to concentrate my mind sufficiently to begin working I turned to this subject as the easiest. But in consequence of my changed mental attitude to it, it became *The Shadow-Line*.[7]

Thus, although Conrad's use of the ship as 'the moral symbol of our life' is constant, his 'changed mental attitude' ensures that *The Shadow-Line* is rather different from those other works that are built on the same set of experiences from 1887–8. In particular, the consciousness of evil and of death that permeates *The Shadow-Line* is not to be found in the much earlier *Youth* (1898). Although the latter is based on a different set of experiences in Conrad's life, like *The Shadow-Line* it is concerned with the passage from youth to maturity. This, together with the far more crucial role allotted to older men such as Captain Giles and Captain Ellis, makes *The Shadow-Line* a far more profound work than stories such as *Falk* and *A Smile of Fortune*, more comprehensive in its view of the human condition, more sombre in tone and outlook.

As with other stories in which Conrad writes of the experiences of a young and inexperienced sea captain, he fully exploits the fascinating tension between isolation and collectivity that the situation affords him. The ship as a symbol of 'our life' functions collectively; as such it can be used to demonstrate the interconnectedness of social life that is—in the everyday world—concealed and unapparent. But Conrad is clear that collectivity is not democracy:

My sensations could not be like those of any other man on board. In that community I stood, like a king in his country, in a class all by myself. I mean an hereditary king, not a mere elected head of a state. (p. 62)

Like the young sea captain in *Falk* and *The Secret Sharer*, the captain in *The Shadow-Line* feels his isolation very sharply, and in all three works this paradoxical feeling of community

[7] See Karl, p. 770.

and isolation offers Conrad the perfect opportunity to explore what are essentially philosophical questions concerning the existence of evil, ageing and the development of self-consciousness, and the nature of morality—its basis and its function.

Among other things *The Shadow-Line* is a study of the dawning of self-consciousness, a self-consciousness engendered by isolation and responsibility:

In the face of that man [Mr Burns], several years, I judged, older than myself, I became aware of what I had left already behind me—my youth. And that was indeed poor comfort. Youth is a fine thing, a mighty power—as long as one does not think of it. I felt I was becoming self-conscious. (p. 55)

This view of the difference between youth and self-conscious maturity has subtly altered from the one offered in *Youth*, in which the perspective of age is given but the emphasis is on the experience of youth. In *The Shadow-Line*, however, it is human maturity, the self-consciousness of the individual concerning his life and place in the scheme of things, that is the point of focus. As in *The Secret Sharer*, the young captain suddenly becomes conscious of his identity as something not given, but (at least in part) still to be constructed. It is not accidental that there are many echoes of *Hamlet*—especially from the great soliloquies—in *The Shadow-Line*. Hamlet's sense of conflicting isolation and responsibility, his shocking perception of the depth of evil in the world, and his subsequent musing upon the place of humanity in a seemingly immoral (or amoral) universe: all of these are direct analogies to the situation of the young captain in *The Shadow-Line*. The corrupting desperation induced by inaction, along with the constant awareness of the presence of disease, are further factors which bind *The Shadow-Line* to *Hamlet*.

In *The Secret Sharer* the young, isolated captain's insecure sense of identity is objectified through the appearance of a 'secret sharer' or double, who represents what he recognizes to be potential courses of development open to him (talking to him on one occasion, the captain feels 'as though I had been faced with my own reflection in the depths of a sombre and immense mirror'). In *The Shadow-Line* the captain actually does see himself in a mirror, and he recognizes that this 'other' is 'not exactly a lonely figure', for

> He had his place in a line of men whom he did not know, of whom he had never heard; but who were fashioned by the same influences, whose souls in relation to their humble life's work had no secrets for him. (p. 53)

Against his isolation, in other words, he is able to set the community of a specific tradition: his captaincy will (like that of the hero of *The Secret Sharer*) involve a search for identity, but one that is not entirely lonely. He imagines a 'sort of composite soul, the soul of command', whispering to him:

> 'You, too!' it seemed to say, 'you, too, shall taste of that peace and that unrest in a searching intimacy with your own self. (p. 53)

Here the isolation and the sense of belonging to a supportive tradition are finely balanced.

That 'searching intimacy with your own self' leads the captain to keep a diary in order to be able to commune with himself (as Conrad had done in the Congo and as his character Razumov, in *Under Western Eyes*, also does when faced with social and moral isolation). Like many of Conrad's sea stories, *The Shadow-Line* is the story of a *test*, a test which enables the protagonist to find the self which, at the start of the tale, he has so conspicuously lost. Like the captain in *The Secret Sharer* he experiences a sense of horrific inadequacy:

> Now I understand that strange sense of insecurity in my past. I always suspected that I might be no good. And here is proof positive, I am shirking it, I am no good. (p. 107)

He is able to pass this test, however—as a result not so much of moral strength as of inculcated modes of behaviour and response, and the help of others. The self-sufficiency of *Youth*—and of youth—has passed. After days drifting in a ship with a diseased crew the captain is ready to accept defeat and death, but the cook Ransome confirms, when asked, that he thinks the captain ought to be on deck. He responds, and we are told that 'The seaman's instinct alone survived whole in my moral dissolution' (p. 109). It is Ransome's catalytic initiative here, along with the accumulated instinct of years as a seaman, that saves the captain, just as it was, earlier, Captain Giles's benevolent prompting that secured his captaincy. Clearly demonstrated here is Conrad's belief in work as a moral agent, building up habits of application that survive moments of personal despair, and forcing the individual to forsake subjectivism and collaborate with other human beings. As Conrad indicated in *Heart of Darkness* and in *Nostromo*, work has a moral force and action a therapeutic value.

Ransome's name is suggestive of Christian forgiveness, and at many points in the text he is described in Christlike terms:

It was a pleasure to look at him. The man positively had grace. (p. 73)

With his serious, clear, grey eyes, his serene temperament, he was a priceless man altogether. Soul as firm as the muscles of his body. (p. 112)

That man noticed everything, attended to everything, shed comfort around him as he moved. (p. 121)

The association is not forced in the text, and is arguably not even dominant so long as we remain concerned only with Ransome as a single character. But the symbolism becomes more apparent when we note how Captain Giles is described much as a benevolent God, who admits that few things are done in town that he cannot see the inside of (p. 38), and who with his 'big paternal fist' (p. 37), and in his general role as protector, functions as a somewhat more sympathetic divinity than the 'Deputy-Neptune' Captain Ellis. As the young captain remarks, we 'wonder what this part of the world would do if you were to leave off looking after it, Captain Giles' (p. 39). We have, moreover, a good steward and a bad steward, and two straightforwardly evil characters: the dead captain, and Hamilton. In a passage of his manuscript (actually forming part of a brief set of typescript pages in the middle of the manuscript) which Conrad had already crossed out in the first copy of the text, the antithesis of good and evil represented by these characters is made explicit:

I could no more forget Captain Giles than Mr. Burns to [sic] forget the late Master of the ship and my extraordinary predecessor.[8]

The work is riddled with biblical or Christian allusions and references: words such as 'sin', 'devil', 'evil spell', 'spiritual strength', 'advent', and 'miracle', recur time and time again, and at one point the captain even feels that he has grown a pair of wings on his shoulders.

This has led many writers to cast doubt on Conrad's disavowal of any supernatural intentions or meaning in his 'Author's Note'. A very early reviewer of the work noted a central ambiguity in it:

The first thing that strikes you is Mr. Conrad's elfin power of mingling the natural with the supernatural . . . all these suggestions, experiences, and episodes might be ascribed *equally* to natural or supernatural causes. The artist reserves his judgment and we reserve ours.[9]

Different readers have argued fervently against accepting Conrad's disavowal of supernatural meaning in his 'Author's Note', but for all the many religious references and motifs in the work I am inclined to accept it, and to take Conrad's word that it is with 'the world of the living' and not that of supernatural forces that *The Shadow-Line* is concerned. In particular, the passage which is for me the most moving part of *The Shadow-Line*, when Ransome asks to be allowed to leave the ship, contains no hint of the supernatural, but celebrates— extraordinarily powerfully—life on earth:

'I must go,' he broke in. 'I have a right!' He gasped and a look of almost savage determination passed over his face. For an instant he was another being. And I saw under the worth and the comeliness of the man the humble reality of things. Life was a boon to him—this precarious hard life—and he was thoroughly alarmed about himself. (p. 129)

---

[8] Joseph Conrad, holograph of *The Shadow-Line*, page in typescript numbered 17.

[9] Unsigned review of *The Shadow-Line*, *Nation* 24 March 1917. Reprinted in Norman Sherry (ed.), *Conrad: The Critical Heritage* (London, Routledge, 1973), p. 307.

At this point in Conrad's writing of the story, his son Borys had certainly enlisted in the army, and this declaration of an unshakeable faith in 'this precarious hard life' has the force of a protest against all that threatens life on earth, a protest as potent in a world full of nuclear weapons as it was in the world of the First World War. Conrad the man accepted the need for Britain to fight the war: Conrad the artist expresses here his horror at its destructiveness.

Conrad certainly contradicted himself when referring to his own religious belief (or lack of it). Reading Zdzisław Najder's description of the many such remarks made by Conrad[10] it is possible to speculate first that Conrad adapted his position according to whom he was talking or writing to, and secondly (as Najder hypothesizes) that Conrad moved closer to an acceptance of (Catholic) Christian belief around 1921—some time after the writing of *The Shadow-Line*. But the following passage (for example) does not read as if it were written by a believer:

'You, too!' it [a 'composite soul of command'] seemed to say, 'you, too, shall taste of that peace and that unrest in a searching intimacy with your own self—obscure as we were and as supreme in the face of all the winds and all the seas, in an immensity that receives no impress, preserves no memories, and keeps no reckoning of lives.' (p. 53)

A passage such as this hints more at the spiritual nullity and impartiality of the elements than at any sort of supernatural agency.

It would be unwise to try to simplify the symbolic meaning of the work and to suggest that alongside the frequent religious references there is a clear division of the characters into sheep and goats. Mr Burns, for example, is frequently associated with satanic references and his name might well be taken to suggest hell-fire. But Burns (whose original, Mr Born, was apparently on rather good terms with the captain of the *Otago* who preceded Conrad) is not a satanic figure in the mould of Kurtz in *Heart of Darkness*. Not only did he stand up to the late mad

---

[10] Zdzisław Najder, *Joseph Conrad: A Chronicle* (Cambridge, Cambridge University Press, 1983). See especially pages 459–60.

captain of the ship who (again, unlike his original) was undoubtedly evil, but in many respects he presents a wonderfully comic figure. Conrad has Dickens's ability to make the pursuit of self-interest amusing (we may think, perhaps, of Mr Guppy in *Bleak House*—a novel Conrad told the readers of *A Personal Record* that he had read 'innumerable times' and for which he had such an intense and unreasoning affection that its very weaknesses were more precious to him than the strengths of other men's work). Mr Burns's unsuccessful attempt to obtain the captaincy for himself may have been wrong, but if it was a sin it was a venial one.

We should not assume that Conrad held many of the items of faith thrust upon later readers by the New Critics: it is quite possible that he never doubted that 'Mr Burns' was much the same person in all the different tales in which he appears, as well as in *The Mirror of the Sea*, in which he is referred to as Mr B——. In each case he is treated as a rather ludicrous and fussy individual, but—as we are told in *The Mirror of the Sea*—'of all my chief officers, the one I trusted most . . . He was worth all his salt'. Thus whereas it is a rather horrific moment in *Heart of Darkness* when Marlow spots Kurtz crawling on hands and knees, when the narrator of *The Shadow-Line* falls over Mr Burns, who is on all fours, the scene is more comic than sinister.

The Shadow-Line certainly suggests that gods can fail. We should note the force of the captain's description of the medicine chest and its contents in religious terms.

I went into the spare cabin where the medicine chest was kept to prepare two doses. I opened it full of faith as a man opens a miraculous shrine. (p. 79)

I believed in it [quinine]. I pinned my faith to it. It would save the men, the ship, break the spell by its medicinal virtue, make time of no account, the weather but a passing worry, and, like a magic powder working against mysterious malefices, secure the first passage of my first command against the evil powers of calms and pestilence. (p. 88)

We can take such ironic passages either as an indication that the wrong supernatural powers are being appealed to, or that any appeal to the supernatural rather than reliance upon the saving powers of hard work and personal integrity is doomed. My preference is for the latter of the two explanations.

Whatever the truth here, it is certainly the case that Christian motifs form a very important part of *The Shadow-Line*—which is no more to say that it is a Christian story than to point to the references to the crossing of the Styx in *Heart of Darkness* is to call that work pagan. (And in *The Shadow-Line* the narrator is handed his papers 'as if they had been my passports for Hades' (p. 7) when he signs off his ship at the beginning of the story.)

Take, for example, the issue of guilt. Like many Conradian heroes, the young captain of *The Shadow-Line* is tormented by guilt—particularly about his failure to check the contents of the medicine chest at the start of the voyage. Some of the references to this guilt seem—to put it mildly—excessive.

And I felt ashamed of having been passed over by the fever which had been preying on every man's strength but mine, in order that my remorse might be the more bitter, the feeling of unworthiness more poignant, and the sense of responsibility heavier to bear. (p. 117)

If, as T. S. Eliot has suggested, Hamlet's equivocation lacks a convincing 'objective correlative',[11] so too does the captain's sense of guilt. He received a letter from the doctor letting him know that the medicine chest had been checked, and the deceitful substitution of the quinine by the previous captain could hardly have been predicted. Besides, the captain appears *not* to feel any guilt for a potentially graver dereliction of duty: his decision to take a sick man with him as mate when specifically warned against doing so by the doctor, thus putting the ship and the whole crew at risk.

An early reviewer of *The Shadow-Line*, Gerald Gould[12], argued that the work suggested a comparison with Coleridge's *The Ancient Mariner*, referring to the presence in both works of ships 'becalmed and bewitched'. There are passages in Conrad's tale which certainly call Coleridge's ghostly ship strongly to mind:

[11] T. S. Eliot, 'Hamlet' (1919). Reprinted in T. S. Eliot, *Selected Essays* (third enlarged edition, reprinted London, Faber, 1969), p. 145.

[12] Gerald Gould, review of *The Shadow-Line*, *New Statesman* 31 March 1917. Reprinted in Sherry 1973, p. 310.

With her anchor at the bow and clothed in canvas to her very trucks, my command seemed to stand as motionless as a model ship set on the gleams and shadows of polished marble. It was impossible to distinguish land from water in the enigmatical tranquillity of the immense forces of the world. (p. 76)

But more than such apparently striking visual parallels, what we can see as 'disproportionate guilt' also links both works. How do we explain this excessive self-deprecation?

The parallel with *The Ancient Mariner* and the importance of Christian motifs in both works suggest that perhaps we are dealing with symbolic portrayals of original sin, a concept that, by relating the condemnation of all mankind to the transgression of Adam and Eve, necessarily brings to mind the issue of disproportionate effects arising from causes unthinkingly initiated. And the Christian doctrine may itself be interpreted as a religious projection of human horror at the devastating results of apparently minor transgressions or omissions.

But a more psychological explanation is possible for the captain's excess of self-blame, and one which involves no supernatural element. His guilt is perhaps more a matter of shock at learning of his own limitations, or of the inescapable limitations of any human attempt to control human destiny, than a genuine recognition of extreme personal culpability. There is a highly ironic touch in the narrative at the point where the captain is waiting for the ship's first movement:

'Won't she answer the helm at all?' I said irritably to the man whose strong brown hands grasping the spokes of the wheel stood out lighted on the darkness; like a symbol of mankind's claim to the direction of its own fate. (p. 76)

Does mankind have a claim to direct its own fate? Or is this the Christian sin of pride, the curse of an Adam who believes God can be dispensed with? *The Shadow-Line* gives no unequivocal answer, but it does suggest that mankind must not rely on magic or benevolent gods, but must act as if we have the key to our own fate. The captain has good luck in getting his command; bad luck in what he experiences on his first voyage as captain; one cannot rule out the blind operation of fate. But he rises above bad luck by dedication and by habits of dogged endurance. Characters such as Hamilton, Burns, and the old captain are subdued and overcome by fate.

An important and characteristically Conradian element here, is suspicion of too much intellectualization, too much consciousness. Again Hamlet, who thinks too much of the event, comes to mind. I quoted earlier the passage in which the captain, newly arrived on his ship, fears that he is becoming self-conscious. At the end of the tale Captain Giles remarks that

a man should stand up to his bad luck, to his mistakes, to his conscience, and all that sort of thing. (pp. 131–2)

And he concludes, shortly after this: 'Precious little rest in life for anybody. Better not think of it.' We can recall other Conradian heroes who think too much of things—the Jim of *Lord Jim*, for instance, who imagines things so perfectly that he cannot act at all, until too late when his imaginings are seen in their true, misleading form. The captain is protected from such Hamlet-like inertia arising from over-cerebration by Ransome: simultaneously Christ-figure and representative of the demands of tradition and collective labour. But the captain is capable of being protected: he has not caught the disease of idleness to which others such as Hamilton have succumbed. Here the fact of his ship's being a sailing (rather than a steam) ship is crucial. Captain Ellis tells him what others are afraid of:

'Afraid of the sails. Afraid of a white crew. Too much trouble. Too much work. Too long out here. Easy life and deck-chairs more their mark.' (p. 31)

We are strongly reminded here of Jim's experience in (appropriately) an Eastern port where, in hospital, he meets white men living unreal dream lives, men who had been thrown there by accident but who had remained as officers of native-owned ships, and who

had now a horror of the home service, with its harder conditions, severer view of duty, and the hazard of stormy oceans. They were attuned to the eternal peace of Eastern sky and sea. They loved short passages, good deck-chairs, large native crews, and the distinction of being white. They shuddered at the thought of hard work, and led precariously easy lives, always on the verge of dismissal, always on the verge of engagement, serving Chinamen, Arabs, half-castes—would have served the devil himself had he made it easy enough. They talked everlastingly of turns of luck . . . and in all they said—in their actions, in their looks, in their persons—could be detected the soft spot, the place of decay, the determination to lounge safely through existence.[13]

This passage reveals that Conrad well understood how colonialism could corrupt those who took advantage of the racial privileges it afforded them, and also that we are given an essential clue to his inner worth and moral potentiality when we are told that the captain of *The Shadow-Line* cannot give his late ship blind loyalty because it is a steamship. This, for Conrad, is a crucial moral indicator—as is too the comment found in a passage in his manuscript but deleted from the published text in which the captain talks of

the nostalgia of a deep-water man for the great open spaces between the continents, for the unbroken horizons of my young days.[14]

As Conrad made clear on repeated occasions, the sailing ship acted as a moral educator of its crew; it demanded hard work and provided a direct contact with the elements rather than labour-saving devices.[15]

There is of course one crucial way in which the 'world' of the ship is quite unlike the larger world of men and women. There are no women on board ship in *The Shadow-Line*. If the ship is a moral symbol of our life then it would, on first sight, appear to be a somewhat masculine, and sexless, life. Again, at first sight, *The Shadow-Line* might seem vulnerable to the feminist criticism that this is a vision of a life rendered ideal by its exclusion of women. It might seem very revealing that the only man in the tale depicted as subject to sexual passion is the late

---

[13] Joseph Conrad, *Lord Jim* (Dent Collected Edition, reprinted London 1974 with new pagination), p. 10. Captain Eliott makes comments resembling this passage in the fifth section of *The End of the Tether*.

[14] Joseph Conrad, holograph of *The Shadow-Line*, p. 103.

[15] A classic source for such opinions is Conrad's *Memorandum* on the scheme for fitting out a sailing ship for the training of Merchant Service officers. This is reprinted in *Last Essays* in the Dent Collected Edition.

captain of the ship who, although married, clearly has had some sort of relationship with

> an awful, mature, white female with rapacious nostrils and a cheaply ill-omened stare in her enormous eyes. She was disguised in some semi-oriental, vulgar, fancy costume. She resembled a low-class medium or one of those women who tell fortunes by cards for half-a-crown. And yet she was striking. A professional sorceress from the slums. It was incomprehensible. There was something awful in the thought that she was the last reflection of the world of passion for the fierce soul which seemed to look at one out of the sardonically savage face of that old seaman. (p. 59)[16]

Do we not have here the image of woman as outsider, as interloper and destroyer in the otherwise stable world of men? Can we not perhaps take this portrayal as an indication that Conrad—consciously or unconsciously—associates sexual passion (on the part of men) and the female sex with moral degeneration and betrayal? Can we not link this description with the allegedly 'fierce mysogynist' John Nieven who, when he hears that the narrator has left his ship, says 'weightily', 'Oh! Aye! I've been thinking it was about time for you to run away home and get married to some silly girl' (p. 6)?

Such a view of *The Shadow-Line* has force, and is not summarily to be dismissed. Recent feminist criticism has established that we cannot ignore the implications of such models or microcosms of human society which are all-male and which depict women as corrupting interlopers.

But woman does appear in *The Shadow-Line* in a transmuted form: as the ship. The newly-appointed captain looks forward to his first meeting with the ship as a lover, and the ship is described as a woman. In a passage in Conrad's manuscript following the (published) description of the ship as 'an enchanted princess' who, 'spellbound, unable to move, to live, to get out into the world (till I came)', is waiting for him, there is an interesting additional comment which concludes with the sentence: 'It was like having been married by proxy to a woman

---

[16] A very similar photograph, found in the ex-captain's fiddle-case along with some jovial and improper verses, is described by the captain-narrator in *Falk*.

one had never seen had never heard of before'.[17] The passage that follows on in the published version of the story also omits a highly significant phrase to be found in Conrad's manuscript:

I discovered how much of a seaman I was, in heart, in mind, and, as it were, physically—a man exclusively of sea and ships; the sea the only world that counted, and the ships [like the women in it,] the test of manliness, of temperament, of courage and fidelity—and of love. (p. 40)

The passage in square brackets appears in Conrad's manuscript[18] but not in the published text. Interestingly, in the manuscript the word 'manliness' is an addition, replacing what looks like 'virility'. (Punctuation also varies slightly in the manuscript.)

Is this a case of woman and sexuality as it were domesticated? Of a male attempt to 'domesticate' the female sex by projecting an idealized view of women (from a man's point of view, that is) on to the ship? We may recall again that the captain, looking forward to seeing his ship for the first time, says, 'I was like a lover looking forward to a meeting.' Is his disastrous first voyage representative of the disillusion of the lover, the concealed judgement of Conrad (or the captain) on women and sexual passion? Should the religious references scattered so liberally through the text remind us that it was Eve who was responsible for the expulsion from Paradise?

To form a complete picture, we need also to consider the force of passages such as the following one:

I knew that, like some rare women, she was one of those creatures whose mere existence is enough to awaken an unselfish delight. One feels that it is good to be in the world in which she has her being. (p. 49)

This could be taken to suggest that the world would be better if women were like well-made ships: beautiful to look at and under the control of an appreciative captain . . . But it does also lend itself to an interpretation that is less critical or reductive of women. We may respond negatively to the use of a word like 'creature', but, that apart, there is something in the

[17] loc. cit., p. 94.   [18] loc. cit., p. 94.

quoted passage to which a modern female reader can perhaps respond favourably.[19]

I would like to conclude with some comment on Conrad's narrative technique in *The Shadow-Line*. In a letter written to Richard Curle in 1923—the year before his own death—Conrad, commenting on a critic of his own work, wrote

My own impression is that what he really meant was that my manner of telling, perfectly devoid of familiarity as between author and reader, aimed essentially at the imtimacy [*sic*] of a personal communication, without any thought for other effects. As a matter of fact, the thought for effects is there all the same (often at the cost of mere directness of narrative), and can be detected in my unconventional grouping and perspective, which is purely temperamental and wherein almost all my 'art' consists. That, I suspect, has been the difficulty the critics felt in classifying it as romantic or realistic. Whereas, as a matter of fact, it is fluid, depending upon grouping (sequence) which shifts, and on the changing lights giving varied effects of perspective.[20]

We have to beware of granting such a *post facto* statement automatic authority—especially as it comes from an author who is notoriously unreliable in comments on his own work. Yet the passage is extremely suggestive, not least with regard to the telling of *The Shadow-Line*. Does not this tale give us the intimacy of a personal communication without familiarity? We feel close, very close, to the narrator, but we do not feel that the work has, in Keats's phrase, 'a palpable design on us'; we do not feel harangued or imposed upon by it.

Let us note a few things about the narrative. First, its origin is very unspecific. We do not know whether it is spoken or written,[21] nor to whom specifically it is addressed. We can

[19] It is perhaps worth noting that both *Falk* and *A Smile of Fortune* have plots that depend upon romantic entanglements. This element is not even hinted at in *The Shadow-Line*.

[20] Richard Curle (ed.), *Conrad to a Friend: 150 Selected Letters from Joseph Conrad to Richard Curle* (London, Sampson Low, Marston and Company, 1928), p. 191. The letter is dated 14 July 1923.

[21] Although, as F. R. Leavis points out, the tale is written in prose that, 'with all its poetic resourcefulness and its finish, keeps closely in touch with speech'. F. R. Leavis, 'The Shadow-Line', *Anna Karenina and Other Essays* (London, Chatto and Windus, 1967), p. 100.

contrast those 'Marlow' stories and novels in which we are clearly given a (framed) *spoken* narrative addressed to a relatively clearly defined group of listeners. This, as has been pointed out, carries certain advantages. The reader feels part of a community of listeners, listening rather than reading, and listening to an Englishman rather than reading the words of a 'foreigner'. But it carries with it certain artificialities as well. One man has to speak for an unnaturally long time, the narration of inner experiences is less convincing—especially when we are meant to assume that they are half-perceived or inadequately verbalized—and the perspective of the narrator is very fixed. The latter problem can be resolved by having a shift from 'young Marlow' to 'old Marlow', and from Marlow to the unnamed, outer narrator (as in *Youth, Heart of Darkness* and *Chance*) or to the 'privileged man' who receives Marlow's narrative in *Lord Jim*. Such shifts have to be handled very carefully if they are not to appear artificial or confusing.

The lack of precise anchoring of the narrative in *The Shadow-Line* allows Conrad the possibility of far more flexibility. We have no written document (apart from the brief extracts from the diary) such as caused Conrad some problems in *Under Western Eyes*. Nor do we have a particular occasion for the delivering of the narrative. We feel an intimate relation with the narrator—so intimate that, at times, it is as if we almost become him.

Of course we can date the narrated events by the reference to Queen Victoria's first jubilee, and we may assume that they are being narrated in 'the present day'—the time of first publication of the story. But the lack of such precise 'placing' information makes the narrative freer—more 'fluid', to use the word Conrad employs in his letter to Curle. It is as if at this late stage in his writing career Conrad is able to dispense with the narrative 'crutches' he has used earlier and to concentrate everything into a sort of pure narrative voice, in which tone, phrasing and sequence take over from the intrusive scaffolding of too specific a setting and narrative mode.

The key words are 'flexibility' and 'economy'; the reader knows what he or she needs to know, in the appropriate order, without ever being bothered by the machinery of the narrative or by its supporting struts and spars.

This is true, too, of Conrad's handling of language in the work. Only at one point are we struck by what F. R. Leavis dubbed Conrad's 'adjectival insistence':[22] 'There was in it an effect of inconceivable terror and of inexpressible mystery.' That shows us Conrad the writer fighting for effect, and not achieving it. Elsewhere we move from scene to scene, from the captain's subjectivity to the outer life of the shore or the ship, without feeling any strain, and we move, too, from thought to speech and dialogue in a similarly free manner.

The Shadow-Line is the masterpiece of Conrad's final period. The view of Conrad's work suggested by Thomas Moser's title, *Achievement and Decline*[23]—the decline starting after *Under Western Eyes*—has much to recommend it. The longer novels written subsequent to *Under Western Eyes* all fail to match the achievement of those great works from *Lord Jim* to *Under Western Eyes*. Nor do Conrad's shorter works written after 1910 stand comparison with the best of those written earlier—with one exception. That exception is *The Shadow-Line*. Had Conrad written nothing but this work, he would still be read today.

[22] F. R. Leavis, *The Great Tradition* (reprinted Harmondsworth, Penguin, 1962), p. 196.
[23] Thomas C. Moser, *Joseph Conrad: Achievement and Decline* (Cambridge, Mass., Harvard University Press, 1957).

NOTE ON THE TEXT

CONRAD started writing *The Shadow-Line* in early 1915, and the date given on the final page of his manuscript is 15 December 1915. (See my explanatory note at the end of this volume concerning Conrad's misdating of the writing of the story in his 'Author's Note'.) It was first published in the *English Review* September 1916–March 1917, and in *Metropolitan Magazine* (New York) in October 1916. First book publication was by J. M. Dent in March 1917.

The present text is substantially that of the Dent Collected Edition (1945). This text was reprinted from the Dent Uniform edition (1923), which was based on the American Sun-Dial edition (Doubleday-Page, 1920).

Conrad's corrected proofs for the 1921 William Heinemann edition are held by the Rosenbach Museum and Library (Philadelphia), which has very kindly provided me with photocopies of them to check against the present text. As this represents the last text of the work with authorial status it is of considerable importance. However, in some instances proof corrections of Conrad's are difficult to read from the photocopies as they 'disappear' into the spine of the book, so some corrections may have escaped me. I have also consulted Conrad's manuscript of the work from a microfilm supplied by the Beinecke Rare Book and Manuscript Library, at Yale University Library.

I am indebted to Yale University Library for permission to quote from Conrad's manuscript of *The Shadow-Line*, the property of the Beinecke Rare Book and Manuscript Library. I am also indebted to the trustees of the Joseph Conrad Estate and to the Rosenbach Museum and Library, Philadelphia, for permission to quote from the page proofs of the 1921 William Heinemann edition of *The Shadow-Line*, as corrected by Joseph Conrad. I would also like to express my thanks to Julia B. Campbell and Marjorie G. Wynne of the Beinecke Rare

Book and Manuscript Library; and to Patricia C. Willis of the Rosenbach Museum and Library. Their help has been very valuable. I am very grateful for my wife's help in checking textual variants.

There are many relatively small variations between different editions of *The Shadow-Line*, often caused by different publishers' house styles. Thus where one edition may have a comma or full stop before direct speech, the other may have a colon. The Heinemann uses hyphens more consistently in terms such as 'side-whiskers' and 'tiffin-time', and its conventions regarding the use of capitals also diverge from those observed in the Dent Collected Edition.

In the present edition I have in general ignored such minor variants, but have concerned myself with three different categories of textual variation.

1. Manuscript material deleted from or changed in published versions. The most important examples of such variation are either mentioned in my Introduction or are given in the Explanatory Notes at the end of this volume.

2. Variations between published texts. In particular, I have compared the Dent Collected Edition text with that of the 1921 Heinemann edition. Significant variations are given below. Of course, although we know that the 1921 Heinemann edition is the last one personally checked by Conrad, we cannot be certain that he is responsible for variants in this text.

3. Conrad's own proof corrections to the 1921 Heinemann edition. These clearly have considerable authority, as not only were they the last textual amendments/corrections made by Conrad to *The Shadow-Line*, but they were made only about five years after Conrad wrote the work.

Two clear errors in the Dent Collected Edition text have been corrected in the present volume:

page 89, line 26: the Dent Collected Edition has 'of this', whereas the Heinemann 1921 edition and Conrad's manuscript have 'this of'.

page 125, line 14: the Dent Collected Edition has 'exercising' whereas both the first English book edition and the 1921 Heinemann edition have 'exorcising'. Neither version appears in Conrad's manuscript, which does not contain the sentence in question.

Variant Readings

1. Variations between the present text and the 1921 William Heinemann edition. I give below page and line references to the *present* volume, followed by the form appearing in the 1921 Heinemann edition.

p. 11, l. 12	'Oh yes, Hamilton!'
p. 13, l. 11	and,
p. 16, l. 4	and I had avoided [this is also the manuscript reading]
p. 17, l. 30	big, benevolent
p. 19, l. 12	'Well, then, I
p. 22, l. 15	asked, laughing
p. 25, l. 2	'Steward,'
l. 28	the lintel of the door.
p. 30, l. 28	after, perhaps,
p. 31, l. 19	they, sir?
p. 32, l. 20	said, with
p. 35, l. 21	spirits, perhaps
p. 37, l. 10	'You have given me away. You have done for me.' [Conrad's manuscript has a question mark after *away*]
p. 38, l. 9	quiet, thick
p. 43, l. 27	concluded, in
p. 48, l. 21	command, and
p. 56, l. 18	face, and
p. 58, l. 2	of sixty-five about [Conrad's manuscript has *of sixty five about*]
p. 79, l. 1	time, though
p. 81, l. 3	news, too
p. 83, l. 17	got, perhaps
l. 19	At least I thought

p. 91, l. 35	'Oh yes,'
p. 92, l. 23	was, perhaps
l. 24	about it, and
l. 30	can do, and
p. 95, l. 19	up, too
p. 96, l. 31	called upon to say [Conrad's manuscript has *there was no need to* which is deleted and replaced by *they were not called to*]
p. 97, l. 1	low, assenting
p. 107, l. 6	them ready
l. 26	black, indeed
p. 113, l. 5	gone too,
p. 125, l. 29	but, mindful

2. Conrad's proof corrections to the 1921 William Heinemann edition, (excluding obvious literals, 'house style' alterations, and corrections/amendments already incorporated in the present edition). I give below details of the page and line references to the *present* edition.

p. xxxvii, l. 6	final *the* at end of line deleted
p. xxxviii, l. 8	'that' altered to ', it'
p. xxxix, l. 27	comma inserted after 'anguish'
p. xl, l. 26	'yet who' altered to 'who yet'
p. 5, l. 23	'these' altered to 'those'
p. 7, l. 18	'were' altered to 'was'
p. 19, l. 22	comma inserted after 'more'
p. 24, l. 7	comma after 'irritating' deleted
l. 27	comma inserted after 'sway'
l. 35	comma inserted after 'open'
p. 25, l. 3	commas inserted after 'absurd' and 'animal'; hyphen inserted between 'hunted' and 'animal'
p. 28, l. 3	exclamation mark after 'Nothing' changed to question mark
p. 33, l. 20	'captain' changed to 'Captain'
p. 34, l. 12	'Duke' changed to 'duke'
p. 37, l. 22–3	commas inserted after 'ahead' and 'were'
p. 39, l. 1	where the Dent has 'those', the Heinemann

	proof has 'them', changed to 'those'. Conrad's manuscript has 'them': see also correction for p. 132
p. 40, l. 32	'I only' changed to 'Only I'
p. 44, l. 35	comma inserted after 'do'
p. 48, l. 26–7	commas inserted after 'but' and 'say'
p. 57, l. 5	comma inserted after 'quarter-deck'
p. 60, l. 17	comma inserted after 'by'
p. 62, l. 32	comma inserted after 'long'
p. 63, l. 23	'head. Whereas' changed to 'head; whereas'
p. 65, l. 33	'resumed' changed to 'résuméd'
p. 66, l. 15	comma deleted after 'Consulate'
p. 70, l. 24	comma inserted after 'argument'
p. 71, l. 11	comma inserted after 'Burns'
p. 76, l. 10	semi-colon after 'darkness' changed to hyphen
p. 78, l. 8	'horizon. The' changed to 'horizon; the'
l. 22	exclamation mark after 'haven't' has been altered, but it is hard to see whether to a full stop or a question mark
p. 79, l. 33	'them. A' changed to 'them—a'
p. 84, l. 22	'men; if' changed to 'men—if'
p. 87, l. 33	comma inserted after 'help'
p. 88, l. 6	'was' changed, probably to 'were'
l. 27	'ever hardly' changed to 'hardly ever'
p. 89, l. 1	question mark after 'discovery' substituted for full stop
p. 91, l. 18	full stop after 'have' changed to question mark
p. 93, l. 12	'indifference. The' changed to 'indifference: the'
p. 96, l. 27	full stop after 'means' changed to question mark
p. 99, l. 24	comma added after 'below'
p. 103, l. 18	'south. Enough' changed to 'south—enough'
p. 107, l. 15	full stop after 'dead' changed to exclamation mark
p. 108, l. 30	comma inserted after 'beat'
p. 115, l. 22	'try' changed to 'tries'
p. 119, l. 9	'mast' changed to 'masts'
l. 20	where the Dent has 'Devil,' the Heinemann

proof has 'devil,' with the comma deleted in a correction

l. 30   'amazing' changed to 'amazingly'

l. 33   comma inserted after 'him'

p. 130, l. 22   comma inserted after 'moment'

p. 132, l. 11   where the Dent has 'those', the Heinemann proof has 'them', corrected to 'those': see also correction for p. 39

SELECT BIBLIOGRAPHY

DENT's Collected Edition, 1946—(based on the Uniform Edition, 1923–8) has all Conrad's works except for *The Inheritors* and *The Nature of a Crime* (which are largely Ford Madox Ford's), *The Sisters*, and the dramatizations. *Congo Diary and Other Uncollected Pieces* (ed. Zdzisław Najder, 1978) contains Conrad's Congo notebooks, *The Sisters, The Nature of a Crime*, and other pieces.

The most important editions of Conrad's letters are as follows: William Blackburn (ed.), *Joseph Conrad: Letters to William Blackwood and David J. Meldrum* (1958), G. Jean-Aubry, *Joseph Conrad: Life and Letters* (1927), Zdzisław Najder (ed.), *Conrad's Polish Background: Letters to and from Polish Friends* (1964), C. T. Watts (ed.), *Joseph Conrad's Letters to R. B. Cunninghame Graham* (1969). There are further collections of letters edited by Richard Curle (1928), Edward Garnett (1928), J. A. Gee and P. J. Sturm (1940), D. B. J. Randall (1968), and G. Jean-Aubry (1930).

There are many biographies and personal memoirs of Conrad; the most important memoirs are those by Jessie Conrad (1926 and 1935), Richard Curle (1928), and Ford Madox Ford (1924), and there are further memoirs by Borys Conrad (1970) and John Conrad (1981). The best biographies of Conrad are those by Jocelyn Baines (1960), G. Jean-Aubry (1957), Bernard Meyer (a 'psychoanalytic' biography, 1967), and Roger Tennant (1981), and there are large critical biographies by Frederick Karl (1979) and Ian Watt (*Conrad in the Nineteenth Century*, 1980).

There are biographically related studies which make substantial use of background or manuscript material of which the most important are J. D. Gordan, *Joseph Conrad: The Making of a Novelist* (1941), Norman Sherry, *Conrad's Eastern World* (1966) and *Conrad's Western World* (1971). There are further relevant studies by Jerry Allen (1965), Edward Crankshaw (1930), Richard Curle (1914), R. R. Hodges (1967), R. L. Mégroz (1931), Gustav Morf (1930 and 1976), J. H. Retinger (1941), and Norman Sherry (1972).

A very large number of critical books have now been published on Conrad. The ones to be most strongly recommended are Jacques Berthoud, *Joseph Conrad: The Major Phase* (1978), H. M. Daleski, *Joseph Conrad: The Way of Dispossession* (1977), A. J. Guerard,

Conrad the Novelist (1958), Jeremy Hawthorn, *Joseph Conrad: Language and Fictional Self-Consciousness* (1979), and E. K. Hay, *The Political Novels of Joseph Conrad* (1963). There are other studies of interest by C. B. Cox (1974), Avrom Fleishman (1967), Douglas Hewitt (1952), Bruce Johnson (1971), Paul Kirschner (1968), and Thomas Moser (1957). There are important essays on Conrad in Graham Hough, *Image and Experience* (1960), J. Hillis Miller, *Poets of Reality* (1966), and Norman Sherry (ed.), *Conrad: The Critical Heritage* (1973) and *Joseph Conrad: A Commemoration* (1976).

On *The Shadow-Line* the following can be particularly recommended: Daniel R. Schwarz, *Conrad: The Later Fiction* (1982), Gary Geddes, *Conrad's Later Novels* (1980), F. R. Leavis, 'The Shadow-Line', in *Anna Karenina and Other Essays* (1967) and Ian Watt, 'Story and Idea in Conrad's *The Shadow-Line*', *Critical Quarterly* 2, Summer 1960.

A CHRONOLOGY OF JOSEPH CONRAD

1857   3 December: Born Józef Teodor Konrad Korzeniowski, of Polish parents in the Ukraine.

1861   His father, poet and translator Apollo Korzeniowski, arrested for patriotic conspiracy.

1862   Conrad's parents exiled to Vologda, Russia; their son accompanies them.

1865   Death of his mother.

1869   Death of Apollo Korzeniowski in Kraków; Conrad comes under the protection of his uncle, Tadeusz Bobrowski.

1874   Leaves Poland for Marseilles to become a trainee seaman with the French merchant navy.

1876   As a 'steward' on the *Sainte-Antoine*, becomes acquainted with Dominic Cervoni (who appears in *The Mirror of the Sea* and *The Arrow of Gold* and is the source for Nostromo, and Peyrol in *The Rover*).

1877   Possibly involved in smuggling arms to the Spanish 'Carlists' from Marseilles.

1878   March: Shoots himself in the chest in Marseilles but is not seriously injured; as a direct result of this suicide attempt his uncle clears his debts. April: Joins his first British ship, the *Mavis*, and later in the same year joins *The Skimmer of the Sea*. Would have become liable for Russian military service if he had stayed with the French merchant navy.

1886   Becomes a British citizen and passes the examination for a Master's certificate.

1887   Is injured on the *Highland Forest* and hospitalized in Singapore.

1887–8   Gets to know the Malay archipelago as an officer of the *Vidar*.

1888   Master of the *Otago*, his only command.

1889   Resigns from the *Otago*, settles briefly in London and begins to write *Almayer's Folly*. Begins a lasting friendship with Marguerite Poradowska.

1890 Works in the Belgian Congo for the Société Anonyme pour le Commerce du Haut-Congo.

1891–3 His pleasantest experience at sea, as an officer of the *Torrens*; meets John Galsworthy, who is among the passengers and becomes a loyal friend.

1893 Autumn: Meets Jessie George.

1894 February: Death of Tadeusz Bobrowski. October: *Almayer's Folly* accepted by Unwin. Meets Edward Garnett, Unwin's reader and an influential literary friend.

1895 *Almayer's Folly* published.

1896 *An Outcast of the Islands* published. Becomes acquainted with H. G. Wells. 24 March: marriage to Jessie George. Begins work on *The Rescue*.

1897 *The Nigger of the 'Narcissus'* published. Meets Henry James and R. B. Cunninghame Graham (to be a close friend and the source for Gould in *Nostromo*).

1898 *Tales of Unrest* ('Karain', 'The Idiots', 'An Outpost of Progress', 'The Return', 'The Lagoon') published. Enters into collaboration with Ford Madox Ford (then Hueffer). Takes over from Ford the lease of a Kentish farmhouse, 'The Pent'. Friendship with Stephen Crane. Borys Conrad born.

1898–9 'Heart of Darkness' serialized in *Blackwood's*.

1899 J. B. Pinker becomes Conrad's literary agent.

1899–1900 *Lord Jim* serialized in *Blackwood's*.

1900 Stephen Crane dies. *Lord Jim* published as a book.

1901 *The Inheritors* (collaboration with Ford) published.

1902 *Youth: and Two Other Stories* ('Youth', 'Heart of Darkness', 'The End of the Tether') published.

1903 *Typhoon: And Other Stories* ('Typhoon', 'Amy Foster', 'Falk', 'Tomorrow') and *Romance* (collaboration with Ford) published.

1904 Jessie Conrad injures her knees and is partially disabled for life. *Nostromo* published.

1906 Meets Arthur Marwood, who becomes his closest friend. John Conrad born. *The Mirror of the Sea* published.

THE SHADOW-LINE

AUTHOR'S NOTE

THIS story, which I admit to be in its brevity a fairly complex piece of work, was not intended to touch on the supernatural. Yet more than one critic has been inclined to take it in that way, seeing in it an attempt on my part to give the fullest scope to my imagination by taking it beyond the confines of the world of the living, suffering humanity. But as a matter of fact my imagination is not made of stuff so elastic as all that. I believe that if I attempted to put the strain of the Supernatural on it it would fail deplorably and exhibit an unlovely gap. But I could never have attempted such a thing, because all my moral and intellectual being is penetrated by an invincible conviction that whatever falls under the dominion of our senses must be in nature and, however exceptional, cannot differ in its essence from all the other effects of the visible and tangible world of which we are a self-conscious part. The world of the living contains enough marvels and mysteries as it is; marvels and mysteries acting upon our emotions and intelligence in ways so inexplicable that it would almost justify the conception of life as an enchanted state. No, I am too firm in my consciousness of the marvellous to be ever fascinated by the mere supernatural, which (take it any way you like) is but a manufactured article, the fabrication of minds insensitive to the intimate delicacies of our relation to the dead and to the living, in their countless multitudes; a desecration of our tenderest memories; an outrage on our dignity.

Whatever my native modesty may be it will never condescend so low as to seek help for my imagination within those vain imaginings common to all ages and that in themselves are enough to fill all lovers of mankind with unutterable sadness. As to the effect of a mental or moral shock on a common mind that is quite a legitimate subject for study and description. Mr. Burns' moral being receives a severe shock in his relations with his late captain, and this in his diseased state turns into a mere superstitious fancy compounded of fear and animosity. This fact is one of the elements of the story, but there is nothing supernatural in it, nothing so to speak from beyond the confines of this world, which in all conscience holds enough mystery and terror in itself.

Perhaps if I had published this tale, which I have had for a long time in my mind, under the title of "First Command" no suggestion of the Supernatural would have been found in it by any impartial reader, critical or otherwise. I will not consider here the origins of the feeling in which its actual title, "The Shadow Line," occurred to my mind. Primarily the aim of this piece of writing was the presentation of certain facts which certainly were associated with the change from youth, care-free and fervent, to the more self-conscious and more poignant period of maturer life. Nobody can doubt that before the supreme trial of a whole generation I had an acute consciousness of the minute and insignificant character of my own obscure experience. There could be no question here of any parallelism. That notion never entered my head. But there was a feeling of identity, though with an enormous difference of scale—as of one single drop measured against the bitter and stormy immensity of an ocean. And this was very natural too. For when we begin to meditate on the meaning of our own past it seems to fill all the world in its profundity and its magnitude. This book was written in the last three months of the year 1916.[*] Of all the subjects of which a writer of tales is more or less conscious within himself this is the only one I found it possible to attempt at the time. The depth and the nature of the mood with which I approached it is best expressed perhaps in the dedication which strikes me now as a most disproportionate thing—as another instance of the overwhelming greatness of our own emotion to ourselves.

This much having been said I may pass on now to a few remarks about the mere material of the story. As to locality it belongs to that part of the Eastern Seas from which I have carried away into my writing life the greatest number of suggestions. From my statement that I thought of this story for a long time under the title of "First Command" the reader may guess that it is concerned with my personal experience. And as a matter of fact it *is* personal experience seen in perspective with the eye of the mind and coloured by that affection one can't help feeling for such events of one's life as one has no reason to be ashamed of. And that affection is as intense (I appeal here to universal experience) as the shame, and almost the anguish with which one remembers some unfortunate occurrences, down to mere mistakes in speech, that have been perpetrated by one in the past. The effect of perspective in memory is to make things loom large because the essentials stand out isolated from their surroundings of insignificant daily facts which have naturally faded out of one's mind. I remember that period of my sea-life with pleasure because begun inauspiciously it turned out in the end a success from a personal point of view, leaving a tangible proof in the terms of the letter the owners of the ship wrote to me two years afterwards when I resigned my command in order to come home. This resignation marked the beginning of another phase of my seaman's life, its terminal phase, if I may say so, which in its own way has coloured another portion of my writings. I didn't know then how near its end my sea-life was, and therefore I felt no sorrow except at parting with the ship. I was sorry also to break my connection with the firm which owned her and who were pleased to receive with friendly kindness and give their confidence to a man who had entered their service in an accidental manner and in very adverse circumstances. Without disparaging the earnestness of my purpose I suspect now that luck had no small part in the success of the trust reposed in me. And one cannot help remembering with pleasure the time when one's best efforts were seconded by a run of luck.

The words "*Worthy of my undying regard*" selected by me for the motto on the title page are quoted from the text of the book itself; and, though one of my critics surmised that they applied to the ship, it is evident from the place where they stand that they refer to the men of that ship's company: complete strangers to their new captain and yet who stood by him so well during those twenty days that seemed to have been passed on the brink of a slow and agonizing destruction. And *that* is the greatest memory of all! For surely it is a great thing to have commanded a handful of men worthy of one's undying regard.

1920.   J. C.

To
Borys and all others
who like himself have crossed
in early youth the shadow-line
of their generation
With Love

THE SHADOW-LINE

· · ·—*D'autres fois, calme plat, grand miroir*
De mon désespoir.

BAUDELAIRE.*

I

ONLY the young have such moments. I don't mean the very young. No. The very young have, properly speaking, no moments. It is the privilege of early youth to live in advance of its days in all the beautiful continuity of hope which knows no pauses and no introspection.

One closes behind one the little gate of mere boyishness—and enters an enchanted garden. Its very shades glow with promise. Every turn of the path has its seduction. And it isn't because it is an undiscovered country.* One knows well enough that all mankind had streamed that way. It is the charm of universal experience from which one expects an uncommon or personal sensation—a bit of one's own.

One goes on recognising the landmarks of the predecessors, excited, amused, taking the hard luck and the good luck together—the kicks and the halfpence, as the saying is—the picturesque common lot that holds so many possibilities for the deserving or perhaps for the lucky. Yes. One goes on. And the time, too, goes on—till one perceives ahead a shadow-line warning one that the region of early youth, too, must be left behind.

This is the period of life in which such moments of

which I have spoken are likely to come. What moments? Why, the moments of boredom, of weariness, of dissatisfaction. Rash moments. I mean moments when the still young are inclined to commit rash actions, such as getting married suddenly or else throwing up a job for no reason.

This is not a marriage story. It wasn't so bad as that with me. My action, rash as it was, had more the character of divorce—almost of desertion. For no reason on which a sensible person could put a finger I threw up my job—chucked my berth—left the ship of which the worst that could be said was that she was a steamship and therefore, perhaps, not entitled to that blind loyalty which. . . . However, it's no use trying to put a gloss on what even at the time I myself half suspected to be a caprice.

It was in an Eastern port. She was an Eastern ship, inasmuch as then she belonged to that port. She traded among dark islands on a blue reef-scarred sea, with the Red Ensign*over the taffrail*and at her masthead a house-flag, also red, but with a green border and with a white crescent in it. For an Arab owned her, and a Syed*at that. Hence the green border on the flag. He was the head of a great House of Straits Arabs, but as loyal a subject of the complex British Empire as you could find east of the Suez Canal. World politics did not trouble him at all, but he had a great occult power amongst his own people.

It was all one to us who owned the ship. He had to employ white men in the shipping part of his business, and many of those he so employed had never set eyes on him from the first to the last day. I myself saw him but once, quite accidentally on a wharf—an old, dark little man blind in one eye, in a snowy robe and yellow slippers. He was having his hand severely kissed by a crowd of Malay pilgrims to whom he had done some favour, in the way of food and money. His alms-giving, I have heard, was most extensive, covering almost the whole Archipelago.* For isn't it said that "The charitable man is the friend of Allah"?

Excellent (and picturesque) Arab owner, about whom one needed not to trouble one's head, a most excellent Scottish ship—for she was that from the keel up—excellent sea-boat, easy to keep clean, most handy in every way, and if it had not been for her internal propulsion, worthy of any man's love, I cherish to this day a profound respect for her memory. As to the kind of trade she was engaged in and the character of my shipmates, I could not have been happier if I had had the life and the men made to my order by a benevolent Enchanter.

And suddenly I left all this. I left it in that, to us, inconsequential manner in which a bird flies away from a comfortable branch. It was as though all unknowing I had heard a whisper or seen something. Well—perhaps! One day I was perfectly right and the next everything was gone—glamour, flavour, interest, contentment—everything. It was one of these moments, you know. The green sickness of late youth*descended on me and carried me off. Carried me off that ship, I mean.

We were only four white men on board, with a large crew of Kalashes*and two Malay petty officers. The Captain stared hard as if wondering what ailed me. But he was a sailor, and he, too, had been young at one time. Presently a smile came to lurk under his thick iron-grey moustache, and he observed that, of course, if I felt I must go he couldn't keep me by main force. And it was arranged that I should be paid off the next morning. As I was going out of the chart-room he added suddenly, in a peculiar, wistful tone, that he hoped I would find what I was so anxious to go and look for. A soft, cryptic utterance which seemed to reach deeper than any diamond-hard tool could have done. I do believe he understood my case.

But the second engineer attacked me differently. He was a sturdy young Scot, with a smooth face and light eyes. His honest red countenance emerged out of the engine-room companion and then the whole robust man, with shirt sleeves turned up, wiping slowly the massive fore-arms with a lump of cotton-waste. And his light eyes expressed bitter distaste, as though our friendship had turned to ashes. He said weightily: "Oh! Aye! I've been thinking it was about time for you to run away home and get married to some silly girl."

It was tacitly understood in the port that John Nieven was a fierce mysogynist; and the absurd character of the sally convinced me that he meant to be nasty—very nasty—had meant to say the most crushing thing he could think of. My laugh sounded deprecatory. Nobody but a friend could be so angry as that. I became a little crestfallen. Our chief engineer also took a characteristic view of my action, but in a kindlier spirit.

He was young, too, but very thin, and with a mist of fluffy brown beard*all round his haggard face. All day long, at sea or in harbour, he could be seen walking hastily up and down the after-deck, wearing an intense, spiritually rapt expression, which was caused by a perpetual consciousness of unpleasant physical sensations in his internal economy. For he was a confirmed dyspeptic.* His view of my case was very simple. He said it was nothing but deranged liver. Of course! He suggested I should stay for another trip and meantime dose myself with a certain patent medicine in which his own belief was absolute. "I'll tell you what I'll do. I'll buy you two bottles, out of my own pocket. There. I can't say fairer than that, can I?"

I believe he would have perpetrated the atrocity (or generosity) at the merest sign of weakening on my part. By that time, however, I was more discontented, disgusted, and dogged than ever. The past eighteen months, so full of new and varied experience, appeared a dreary, prosaic waste of days. I felt—how shall I express it?—that there was no truth to be got out of them.

What truth? I should have been hard put to it to explain. Probably, if pressed, I would have burst into tears simply. I was young enough for that.

Next day the Captain and I transacted our business in the Harbour Office. It was a lofty, big, cool, white room, where the screened light of day glowed serenely. Everybody in it—the officials, the public—were in white. Only the heavy polished desks gleamed darkly in a central avenue, and some papers lying on them were blue. Enormous punkahs* sent from on high a gentle draught through that immaculate interior and upon our perspiring heads.

The official behind the desk we approached grinned amiably and kept it up till, in answer to his perfunctory question, "Sign off and on again?" my Captain answered, "No! Signing off for good." And then his grin vanished in sudden solemnity. He did not look at me again till he handed me my papers with a sorrowful expression, as if they had been my passports for Hades.*

While I was putting them away he murmured some question to the Captain, and I heard the latter answer good-humouredly:

"No. He leaves us to go home."

"Oh!" the other exclaimed, nodding mournfully over my sad condition.

I didn't know him outside the official building, but he leaned forward over the desk to shake hands with me, compassionately, as one would with some poor devil going out to be hanged; and I am afraid I performed my part ungraciously, in the hardened manner of an impenitent criminal.

No homeward-bound mail-boat was due for three or four days. Being now a man without a ship, and having for a time broken my connection with the sea—become, in fact, a mere potential passenger—it would have been more appropriate perhaps if I had gone to stay at an hotel. There it was, too, within a stone's throw of the Harbour Office, low, but somehow palatial, displaying its white, pillared pavilions surrounded by trim grass plots. I would have felt a passenger indeed in there! I gave it a hostile glance and directed my steps towards the Officers' Sailors' Home.

I walked in the sunshine, disregarding it, and in the shade of the big trees on the Esplanade without enjoying it. The heat of the tropical East descended through the leafy boughs, enveloping my thinly clad body, clinging to my rebellious discontent,* as if to rob it of its freedom.

The Officers' Home was a large bungalow with a wide verandah and a curiously suburban-looking little garden of bushes and a few trees between it and the street. That institution partook somewhat of the character of a residental club, but with a slightly Governmental flavour about it, because it was administered by the Harbour Office. Its manager was officially styled Chief Steward. He was an unhappy, wizened little man, who if put into a jockey's rig would have looked the part to perfection. But it was obvious that at some time or other in his life, in some capacity or other, he had been connected with the sea. Possibly in the comprehensive capacity of a failure.

I should have thought his employment a very easy one, but he used to affirm for some reason or other that his job would be the death of him some day. It was rather mysterious. Perhaps everything naturally was too much trouble for him. He certainly seemed to hate having people in the house.

On entering it I thought he must be feeling pleased. It was as still as a tomb. I could see no one in the living rooms; and the verandah, too, was empty, except for a man at the far end dozing prone in a long chair. At the noise of my footsteps he opened one horribly fish-like eye. He was a stranger to me. I retreated from there, and, crossing the dining-room—a very bare apartment with a motionless punkah hanging over the centre table—I knocked at a door labelled in black letters: "Chief Steward."

The answer to my knock being a vexed and doleful plaint: "Oh, dear! Oh, dear! What is it now?" I went in at once.

It was a strange room to find in the tropics. Twilight and stuffiness reigned in there. The fellow had hung enormously ample, dusty, cheap lace curtains over his windows, which were shut. Piles of cardboard boxes, such as milliners*and dressmakers use in Europe, cumbered the corners; and by some means he had procured for himself the sort of furniture that might have come out of a respectable parlour in the East End of London*—a horsehair sofa, arm-chairs of the same. I glimpsed grimy antimacassars* scattered over that horrid upholstery, which was awe-inspiring, insomuch that one could not guess what mysterious accident, need, or fancy had collected it there. Its owner had taken off his tunic, and in white trousers and a thin short-sleeved singlet prowled behind the chair-backs nursing his meagre elbows.

An exclamation of dismay escaped him when he heard that I had come for a stay; but he could not deny that there were plenty of vacant rooms.

"Very well. Can you give me the one I had before?"

He emitted a faint moan from behind a pile of cardboard boxes on the table, which might have contained gloves or handkerchiefs or neckties. I wonder what the fellow did keep in them? There was a smell of decaying coral, or Oriental dust, of zoological specimens in that den of his. I could only see the top of his head and his unhappy eyes levelled at me over the barrier.

"It's only for a couple of days," I said, intending to cheer him up.

"Perhaps you would like to pay in advance?" he suggested eagerly.

"Certainly not!" I burst out directly I could speak. "Never heard of such a thing! This is the most infernal cheek. . . ."

He had seized his head in both hands—a gesture of despair which checked my indignation.

"Oh, dear! Oh, dear! Don't fly out like this. I am asking everybody."

"I don't believe it," I said bluntly.

"Well, I am going to. And if you gentlemen all agreed to pay in advance I could make Hamilton pay up too. He's always turning up ashore dead broke, and even when he has some money he won't settle his bills. I don't know what to do with him. He swears at me and tells me I can't chuck a white man out into the street here. So if you only would. . . ."

I was amazed. Incredulous too. I suspected the fellow of gratuitous impertinence. I told him with marked emphasis that I would see him and Hamilton hanged first, and requested him to conduct me to my room with no more of his nonsense. He produced then a key from somewhere and led the way out of his lair, giving me a vicious sidelong look in passing.

"Any one I know staying here?" I asked him before he left my room.

He had recovered his usual pained impatient tone, and said that Captain Giles was there, back from a Solo Sea trip.* Two other guests were staying also. He paused. And, of course, Hamilton, he added.

"Oh, yes! Hamilton," I said, and the miserable creature took himself off with a final groan.

His impudence still rankled when I came into the dining-room at tiffin time.* He was there on duty overlooking the Chinamen servants. The tiffin was laid on one end only of the long table, and the punkah was stirring the hot air lazily—mostly above a barren waste of polished wood.

We were four around the cloth. The dozing stranger from the chair was one. Both his eyes were partly opened now, but they did not seem to see anything. He was supine. The dignified person next him, with short side whiskers and a carefully scraped chin, was, of course, Hamilton. I have never seen any one so full of dignity for the station in life Providence had been pleased to place him in. I had been told that he regarded me as a rank outsider. He raised not only his eyes, but his eyebrows as well, at the sound I made pulling back my chair.

Captain Giles was at the head of the table. I exchanged a few words of greeting with him and sat down on his left. Stout and pale, with a great shiny dome of a bald forehead and prominent brown eyes, he might have been anything but a seaman. You would not have been surprised to learn that he was an architect. To me (I know how absurd it is) he looked like a church-warden. He had the appearance of a man from whom you would expect sound advice, moral sentiments, with perhaps a platitude or two thrown in on occasion, not from a desire to dazzle, but from honest conviction.

Though very well known and appreciated in the shipping world, he had no regular employment. He did not want it. He had his own peculiar position. He was an expert. An expert in—how shall I say it?— in intricate navigation. He was supposed to know more about remote and imperfectly charted parts of the Archipelago than any man living. His brain must have been a perfect warehouse of reefs, positions, bearings, images of headlands, shapes of obscure coasts, aspects of innumerable islands, desert and otherwise. Any ship, for instance, bound on a trip to Palawan*or somewhere that way would have Captain Giles on board, either in temporary command or "to assist the master." It was said that he had a retaining fee from a wealthy firm of Chinese steamship owners, in view of such services. Besides, he was always ready to relieve any man who wished to take a spell ashore for a time. No owner was ever known to object to an arrangement of that sort. For it seemed to be the established opinion at the port that Captain Giles was as good as the best, if not a little better. But in Hamilton's view he was an "outsider". I believe that for Hamilton the generalisation "outsider" covered the whole lot of us; though I suppose that he made some distinctions in his mind.

I didn't try to make conversation with Captain Giles, whom I had not seen more than twice in my life. But, of course, he knew who I was. After a while, inclining his big shiny head my way, he addressed me first in his friendly fashion. He presumed from seeing me there, he said, that I had come ashore for a couple of days' leave.

He was a low-voiced man. I spoke a little louder, saying that: No—I had left the ship for good.

"A free man for a bit," was his comment.

"I suppose I may call myself that—since eleven o'clock," I said.

Hamilton had stopped eating at the sound of our voices. He laid down his knife and fork gently, got up, and muttering something about "this infernal heat cutting one's appetite," went out of the room. Almost immediately we heard him leave the house down the verandah steps.

On this Captain Giles remarked easily that the fellow had no doubt gone off to look after my old job. The Chief Steward, who had been leaning against the wall, brought his face of an unhappy goat nearer to the table and addressed us dolefully. His object was to unburden himself of his eternal grievance against Hamilton. The man kept him in hot water with the Harbour Office as to the state of his accounts. He wished to goodness he would get my job, though in truth what would it be? Temporary relief at best.

I said: "You needn't worry. He won't get my job. My successor is on board already."

He was surprised, and I believe his face fell a little at the news. Captain Giles gave a soft laugh. We got up and went out on the verandah, leaving the supine stranger to be dealt with by the Chinamen. The last thing I saw they had put a plate with a slice of pine-apple on it before him and stood back to watch what would happen. But the experiment seemed a failure. He sat insensible.

It was imparted to me in a low voice by Captain

Giles that this was an officer of some Rajah's*yacht
which had come into our port to be dry-docked. Must
have been "seeing life" last night, he added, wrinkling
his nose in an intimate, confidential way which pleased
me vastly. For Captain Giles had prestige. He was
credited with wonderful adventures and with some
mysterious tragedy in his life. And no man had a word
to say against him. He continued:

"I remember him first coming ashore here some
years ago. Seems only the other day. He was a nice
boy. Oh! these nice boys!"

I could not help laughing aloud. He looked startled,
then joined in the laugh. "No! No! I didn't mean
that," he cried. "What I meant is that some of them
do go soft mighty quick out here."

Jocularly I suggested the beastly heat as the first
cause. But Captain Giles disclosed himself possessed
of a deeper philosophy. Things out East were made
easy for white men. That was all right. The difficulty
was to go on keeping white, and some of these nice
boys did not know how. He gave me a searching
look, and in a benevolent, heavy-uncle manner asked
point blank:

"Why did you throw up your berth?"

I became angry all of a sudden; for you can understand how exasperating such a question was to a man
who didn't know. I said to myself that I ought to shut
up that moralist; and to him aloud I said with challeng-
ing politeness:

"Why . . . ? Do you disapprove?"

He was too disconcerted to do more than mutter
confusedly: "I! . . . In a general way . . ."
and then gave me up. But he retired in good order,
under the cover of a heavily humorous remark that he,
too, was getting soft, and that this was his time for

taking his little siesta*—when he was on shore. "Very bad habit. Very bad habit."

The simplicity of the man would have disarmed a touchiness even more youthful than mine. So when next day at tiffin he bent his head towards me and said that he had met my late Captain last evening, adding in an undertone: "He's very sorry you left. He had never had a mate that suited him so well," I answered him earnestly, without any affectation, that I certainly hadn't been so comfortable in any ship or with any commander in all my sea-going days.

"Well—then," he murmured.

"Haven't you heard, Captain Giles, that I intend to go home?"

"Yes," he said benevolently. "I have heard that sort of thing so often before."

"What of that?" I cried. I thought he was the most dull, unimaginative man I had ever met. I don't know what more I would have said, but the much-belated Hamilton came in just then and took his usual seat. So I dropped into a mumble.

"Anyhow, you shall see it done this time."

Hamilton, beautifully shaved, gave Captain Giles a curt nod, but didn't even condescend to raise his eyebrows at me; and when he spoke it was only to tell the Chief Steward that the food on his plate wasn't fit to be set before a gentleman. The individual addressed seemed much too unhappy to groan. He only cast his eyes up to the punkah and that was all.

Captain Giles and I got up from the table, and the stranger next to Hamilton followed our example, manœuvring himself to his feet with difficulty. He, poor fellow, not because he was hungry but I verily believe only to recover his self-respect, had tried to put some of that unworthy food into his mouth. But after dropping his fork twice and generally making a failure of it, he had sat still with an air of intense mortification combined with a ghastly glazed stare. Both Giles and I avoided looking his way at table.

On the verandah he stopped short on purpose to address to us anxiously a long remark which I failed to understand completely. It sounded like some horrible unknown language. But when Captain Giles, after only an instant for reflection, answered him with homely friendliness, "Aye, to be sure. You are right there," he appeared very much gratified indeed, and went away (pretty straight too) to seek a distant long chair.

"What was he trying to say?" I asked with disgust.

"I don't know. Mustn't be down too much on a fellow. He's feeling pretty wretched, you may be sure; and to-morrow he'll feel worse yet."

Judging by the man's appearance it seemed impossible. I wondered what sort of complicated debauch had reduced him to that unspeakable condition. Captain Giles' benevolence was spoiled by a curious air of complacency which I disliked. I said with a little laugh:

"Well, he will have you to look after him."

He made a deprecatory gesture, sat down, and took up a paper. I did the same. The papers were old and uninteresting, filled up mostly with dreary stereo-typed descriptions of Queen Victoria's first jubilee celebrations.* Probably we should have quickly fallen into a tropical afternoon doze if it had not been for Hamilton's voice raised in the dining-room. He was finishing his tiffin there. The big double doors stood wide open permanently, and he could not have had any idea how near to the doorway our chairs were placed. He was heard in a loud, supercilious tone answering some statement ventured by the Chief Steward.

"I am not going to be rushed into anything. They will be glad enough to get a gentleman I imagine. There is no hurry."

A loud whispering from the steward succeeded and then again Hamilton was heard with even intenser scorn.

"What? That young ass who fancies himself for having been chief mate with Kent so long? . . . Preposterous."

Giles and I looked at each other. Kent being the name of my late commander, Captain Giles' whisper, "He's talking of you," seemed to me sheer waste of breath. The Chief Steward must have stuck to his point whatever it was, because Hamilton was heard again more supercilious, if possible, and also very emphatic:

"Rubbish, my good man! One doesn't *compete* with a rank outsider like that. There's plenty of time."

Then there was pushing of chairs, footsteps in the next room, and plaintive expostulations from the Steward, who was pursuing Hamilton, even out of doors through the main entrance.

"That's a very insulting sort of man," remarked Captain Giles—superfluously, I thought. "Very insulting. You haven't offended him in some way, have you?"

"Never spoke to him in my life," I said grumpily. "Can't imagine what he means by competing. He has been trying for my job after I left—and didn't get it. But that isn't exactly competition."

Captain Giles balanced his big benevolent head thoughtfully. "He didn't get it," he repeated very slowly. "No, not likely either, with Kent. Kent is no end sorry you left him. He gives you the name of a good seaman too."

I flung away the paper I was still holding. I sat

up, I slapped the table with my open palm. I wanted to know why he would keep harping on that, my absolutely private affair. It was exasperating, really.

Captain Giles silenced me by the perfect equanimity of his gaze. "Nothing to be annoyed about," he murmured reasonably, with an evident desire to soothe the childish irritation he had aroused. And he was really a man of an appearance so inoffensive that I tried to explain myself as much as I could. I told him that I did not want to hear any more about what was past and gone. It had been very nice while it lasted, but now it was done with I preferred not to talk about it or even think about it. I had made up my mind to go home.

He listened to the whole tirade in a particular, lending-the-ear attitude, as if trying to detect a false note in it somewhere; then straightened himself up and appeared to ponder sagaciously over the matter.

"Yes. You told me you meant to go home. Anything in view there?"

Instead of telling him that it was none of his business I said sullenly:

"Nothing that I know of."

I had indeed considered that rather blank side of the situation I had created for myself by leaving suddenly my very satisfactory employment. And I was not very pleased with it. I had it on the tip of my tongue to say that common sense had nothing to do with my action, and that therefore it didn't deserve the interest Captain Giles seemed to be taking in it. But he was puffing at a short wooden pipe now, and looked so guileless, dense, and commonplace, that it seemed hardly worth while to puzzle him either with truth or sarcasm.

He blew a cloud of smoke, then surprised me by a very abrupt: "Paid your passage money yet?"

Overcome by the shameless pertinacity of a man to

whom it was rather difficult to be rude, I replied with
exaggerated meekness that I had not done so yet. I
thought there would be plenty of time to do that to-
morrow.

And I was about to turn away, withdrawing my
privacy from his fatuous, objectless attempts to test
what sort of stuff it was made of, when he laid down his
pipe in an extremely significant manner, you know, as if
a critical moment had come, and leaned sideways over
the table between us.

"Oh! You haven't yet!" He dropped his voice
mysteriously. "Well, then I think you ought to know
that there's something going on here."

I had never in my life felt more detached from all
earthly goings on. Freed from the sea for a time, I
preserved the sailor's consciousness of complete independence from all land affairs. How could they concern me? I gazed at Captain Giles' animation with
scorn rather than with curiosity.

To his obviously preparatory question whether our
steward had spoken to me that day I said he hadn't.
And what's more he would have had precious little encouragement if he had tried to. I didn't want the
fellow to speak to me at all.

Unrebuked by my petulance, Captain Giles, with
an air of immense sagacity, began to tell me a minute
tale about a Harbour Office peon.* It was absolutely
pointless. A peon was seen walking that morning
on the verandah with a letter in his hand. It was in an
official envelope. As the habit of these fellows is, he had
shown it to the first white man he came across. That
man was our friend in the arm-chair. He, as I knew,
was not in a state to interest himself in any sublunary
matters. He could only wave the peon away. The
peon then wandered on along the verandah and came

upon Captain Giles, who was there by an extraordinary chance. . . .

At this point he stopped with a profound look. The letter, he continued, was addressed to the Chief Steward. Now what could Captain Ellis, the Master Attendant, want to write to the Steward for? The fellow went every morning, anyhow, to the Harbour Office with his report, for orders or what not. He hadn't been back more than an hour before there was an office peon chasing him with a note. Now what was that for?

And he began to speculate. It was not for this—and it could not be for that. As to that other thing it was unthinkable.

The fatuousness of all this made me stare. If the man had not been somehow a sympathetic personality I would have resented it like an insult. As it was, I felt only sorry for him. Something remarkably earnest in his gaze prevented me from laughing in his face. Neither did I yawn at him. I just stared.

His tone became a shade more mysterious. Directly the fellow (meaning the Steward) got that note he rushed for his hat and bolted out of the house. But it wasn't because the note called him to the Harbour Office. He didn't go there. He was not absent long enough for that. He came darting back in no time, flung his hat away, and raced about the dining-room moaning and slapping his forehead. All these exciting facts and manifestations had been observed by Captain Giles. He had, it seems, been meditating upon them ever since.

I began to pity him profoundly. And in a tone which I tried to make as little sarcastic as possible I said that I was glad he had found something to occupy his morning hours.

With his disarming simplicity he made me observe, as if it were a matter of some consequence, how strange it was that he should have spent the morning indoors at all. He generally was out before tiffin, visiting various offices, seeing his friends in the harbour, and so on. He had felt out of sorts somewhat on rising. Nothing much. Just enough to make him feel lazy.

All this with a sustained, holding stare which, in conjunction with the general inanity of the discourse, conveyed the impression of mild, dreary lunacy. And when he hitched his chair a little and dropped his voice to the low note of mystery, it flashed upon me that high professional reputation was not necessarily a guarantee of sound mind.

It never occurred to me then that I didn't know in what soundness of mind exactly consisted and what a delicate and, upon the whole, unimportant matter it was. With some idea of not hurting his feelings I blinked at him in an interested manner. But when he proceeded to ask me mysteriously whether I remembered what had passed just now between that Steward of ours and "that man Hamilton," I only grunted sour assent and turned away my head.

"Aye. But do you remember every word?" he insisted tactfully.

"I don't know. It's none of my business," I snapped out, consigning, moreover, the Steward and Hamilton aloud to eternal perdition.

I meant to be very energetic and final, but Captain Giles continued to gaze at me thoughtfully. Nothing could stop him. He went on to point out that my personality was involved in that conversation. When I tried to preserve the semblance of unconcern he became positively cruel. I heard what the man had said? Yes? What did I think of it then?—he wanted to know.

Captain Giles' appearance excluding the suspicion of mere sly malice, I came to the conclusion that he was simply the most tactless idiot on earth. I almost despised myself for the weakness of attempting to enlighten his common understanding. I started to explain that I did not think anything whatever. Hamilton was not worth a thought. What such an offensive loafer . . .— "Aye! that he is," interjected Captain Giles—. . . thought or said was below any decent man's contempt, and I did not propose to take the slightest notice of it.

This attitude seemed to me so simple and obvious that I was really astonished at Giles giving no sign of assent. Such perfect stupidity was almost interesting. "What would you like me to do?" I asked laughing. "I can't start a row with him because of the opinion he has formed of me. Of course, I've heard of the contemptuous way he alludes to me. But he doesn't intrude his contempt on my notice. He has never expressed it in my hearing. For even just now he didn't know we could hear him. I should only make myself ridiculous."

That hopeless Giles went on puffing at his pipe moodily. All at once his face cleared, and he spoke.

"You missed my point."

"Have I? I am very glad to hear it," I said.

With increasing animation he stated again that I had missed his point. Entirely. And in a tone of growing self-conscious complacency he told me that few things escaped his attention, and he was rather used to think them out, and generally from his experience of life and men arrived at the right conclusion.

This bit of self-praise, of course, fitted excellently the laborious inanity of the whole conversation. The whole thing strengthened in me that obscure feeling of life being but a waste of days, which, half-unconsciously, had driven me out of a comfortable berth, away from men I liked, to flee from the menace of emptiness . . . and to find inanity at the first turn. Here was a man of recognised character and achievement disclosed as an absurd and dreary chatterer. And it was probably like this everywhere—from east to west, from the bottom to the top of the social scale.

A great discouragement fell on me. A spiritual drowsiness. Giles' voice was going on complacently; the very voice of the universal hollow conceit. And I was no longer angry with it. There was nothing original, nothing new, startling, informing to expect from the world: no opportunities to find out something about oneself, no wisdom to acquire, no fun to enjoy. Everything was stupid and overrated, even as Captain Giles was. So be it.

The name of Hamilton suddenly caught my ear and roused me up.

"I thought we had done with him," I said, with the greatest possible distaste.

"Yes. But considering what we happened to hear just now I think you ought to do it."

"Ought to do it?" I sat up bewildered. "Do what?"

Captain Giles confronted me very much surprised.

"Why! Do what I have been advising you to try. You go and ask the Steward what was there in that letter from the Harbour Office. Ask him straight out."

I remained speechless for a time. Here was something unexpected and original enough to be altogether incomprehensible. I murmured, astounded:

"But I thought it was Hamilton that you . . ."

"Exactly. Don't you let him. You do what I tell you. You tackle that Steward. You'll make him

jump, I bet," insisted Captain Giles, waving his smouldering pipe impressively at me.   Then he took three
rapid puffs at it.

His aspect of triumphant acuteness was indescribable.
Yet the man remained a strangely sympathetic creature.
Benevolence radiated from him ridiculously, mildly,
impressively.   It was irritating, too.   But I pointed
out coldly, as one who deals with the incomprehensible,
that I didn't see any reason to expose myself to a snub
from the fellow.   He was a very unsatisfactory steward
and a miserable wretch besides, but I would just as soon
think of tweaking his nose.

"'Tweaking his nose," said Captain Giles in a scan-
dalised tone.   "Much use it would be to you."

That remark was so irrelevant that one could make
no answer to it.   But the sense of the absurdity was
beginning at last to exercise its well-known fascination.
I felt I must not let the man talk to me any more.   I
got up, observing curtly that he was too much for me—
that I couldn't make him out.

Before I had time to move away he spoke again in a
changed tone of obstinacy and puffing nervously at his
pipe.

"Well—he's a—no account cuss—anyhow.   You
just—ask him.   That's all."

That new manner impressed me—or rather made me
pause.   But sanity asserting its sway at once I left the
verandah after giving him a mirthless smile.   In a few
strides I found myself in the dining-room, now cleared
and empty.   But during that short time various
thoughts occurred to me, such as: that Giles had been
making fun of me, expecting some amusement at my
expense; that I probably looked silly and gullible;
that I knew very little of life.   .   .   .

The door facing me across the dining-room flew open

to my extreme surprise. It was the door inscribed with the word "Steward" and the man himself ran out of his stuffy Philistinish lair*in his absurd hunted animal manner, making for the garden door.

To this day I don't know what made me call after him: "I say! Wait a minute." Perhaps it was the sidelong glance he gave me; or possibly I was yet under the influence of Captain Giles' mysterious earnestness. Well, it was an impulse of some sort; an effect of that force somewhere within our lives which shapes them this way or that.* For if these words had not escaped from my lips (my will had nothing to do with that) my existence would, to be sure, have been still a seaman's existence, but directed on now to me utterly inconceivable lines.

No. My will had nothing to do with it. Indeed, no sooner had I made that fateful noise than I became extremely sorry for it. Had the man stopped and faced me I would have had to retire in disorder. For I had no notion to carry out Captain Giles' idiotic joke, either at my own expense or at the expense of the Steward.

But here the old human instinct of the chase came into play. He pretended to be deaf, and I, without thinking a second about it, dashed along my own side of the dining table and cut him off at the very door.

"Why can't you answer when you are spoken to?" I asked roughly.

He leaned against the side of the door. He looked extremely wretched. Human nature is, I fear, not very nice right through. There are ugly spots in it. I found myself growing angry, and that, I believe, only because my quarry looked so woe-begone. Miserable beggar!

I went for him without more ado. "I understand there was an official communication to the Home from the Harbour Office this morning. Is that so?"

Instead of telling me to mind my own business, as he might have done, he began to whine with an undertone of impudence. He couldn't see me anywhere this morning. He couldn't be expected to run all over the town after me.

"Who wants you to?" I cried. And then my eyes became opened to the inwardness of things and speeches the triviality of which had been so baffling and tiresome.

I told him I wanted to know what was in that letter. My sternness of tone and behaviour was only half assumed. Curiosity can be a very fierce sentiment—at times.

He took refuge in a silly, muttering sulkiness. It was nothing to me, he mumbled. I had told him I was going home. And since I was going home he didn't see why he should. . . .

That was the line of his argument, and it was irrelevant enough to be almost insulting. Insulting to one's intelligence, I mean.

In that twilight region between youth and maturity, in which I had my being then, one is peculiarly sensitive to that kind of insult. I am afraid my behaviour to the Steward became very rough indeed. But it wasn't in him to face out anything or anybody. Drug habit or solitary tippling, perhaps. And when I forgot myself so far as to swear at him he broke down and began to shriek.

I don't mean to say that he made a great outcry. It was a cynical shrieking confession, only faint—piteously faint. It wasn't very coherent either, but sufficiently so to strike me dumb at first. I turned my eyes from him in righteous indignation, and perceived Captain Giles in the verandah doorway surveying quietly the scene, his own handiwork, if I may express it in that way. His smouldering black pipe was very noticeable in his big, paternal fist. So, too, was the glitter of his heavy gold watch-chain across the breast of his white tunic. He exhaled an atmosphere of virtuous sagacity thick enough for any innocent soul to fly to confidently. I flew to him.

"You would never believe it," I cried. "It was a notification that a master is wanted for some ship. There's a command apparently going about and this fellow puts the thing in his pocket."

The Steward screamed out in accents of loud despair, "You will be the death of me!"

The mighty slap he gave his wretched forehead was very loud, too. But when I turned to look at him he was no longer there. He had rushed away somewhere out of sight. This sudden disappearance made me laugh.

This was the end of the incident—for me. Captain Giles, however, staring at the place where the Steward had been, began to haul at his gorgeous gold chain till at last the watch came up from the deep pocket like solid truth from a well. Solemnly he lowered it down again and only then said:

"Just three o'clock. You will be in time—if you don't lose any, that is."

"In time for what?" I asked.

"Good Lord! For the Harbour Office. This must be looked into."

Strictly speaking, he was right. But I've never had much taste for investigation, for showing people up and all that, no doubt, ethically meritorious kind of work. And my view of the episode was purely ethical. If any one had to be the death of the Steward I didn't see why it shouldn't be Captain Giles himself, a man of age and standing, and a permanent resident. Whereas I, in comparison, felt myself a mere bird of passage in that port. In fact, it might have been said that I had al-

ready broken off my connection. I muttered that I
didn't think—it was nothing to me. . . .

"Nothing!" repeated Captain Giles, giving some
signs of quiet, deliberate indignation. "Kent warned
me you were a peculiar young fellow. You will tell me
next that a command is nothing to you—and after all
the trouble I've taken, too!"

"The trouble!" I murmured, uncomprehending.
What trouble? All I could remember was being
mystified and bored by his conversation for a solid hour
after tiffin. And he called that taking a lot of trouble.

He was looking at me with a self-complacency which
would have been odious in any other man. All at
once, as if a page of a book had been turned over disclosing a word which made plain all that had gone before, I perceived that this matter had also another than
an ethical aspect.

And still I did not move. Captain Giles lost his
patience a little. With an angry puff at his pipe he
turned his back on my hesitation.

But it was not hesitation on my part. I had been, if
I may express myself so, put out of gear mentally. But
as soon as I had convinced myself that this stale,
unprofitable world of my discontent*contained such a
thing as a command to be seized, I recovered my
powers of locomotion.

It's a good step from the Officers' Home to the
Harbour Office; but with the magic word "Command" in
my head I found myself suddenly on the quay as if trans-
ported there in the twinkling of an eye, before a portal
of dressed white stone above a flight of shallow white
steps.

All this seemed to glide towards me swiftly. The
whole great roadstead to the right was just a mere
flicker of blue, and the dim cool hall swallowed me up

out of the heat and glare of which I had not been aware till the very moment I passed in from it.

The broad inner staircase insinuated itself under my feet somehow. Command is a strong magic. The first human beings I perceived distinctly since I had parted with the indignant back of Captain Giles was the crew of the harbour steam-launch lounging on the spacious landing about the curtained archway of the shipping office.

It was there that my buoyancy abandoned me. The atmosphere of officialdom would kill anything that breathes the air of human endeavour, would extinguish hope and fear alike in the supremacy of paper and ink. I passed heavily under the curtain which the Malay coxswain*of the harbour launch raised for me. There was nobody in the office except the clerks, writing in two industrious rows. But the head shipping-master hopped down from his elevation and hurried along on the thick mats to meet me in the broad central passage.

He had a Scottish name, but his complexion was of a rich olive hue, his short beard was jet black, and his eyes, also black, had a languishing expression. He asked confidentially:

"You want to see Him?"

All lightness of spirit and body having departed from me at the touch of officialdom, I looked at the scribe without animation and asked in my turn wearily:

"What do you think? Is it any use?"

"My goodness! He has asked for you twice to-day."

This emphatic He was the supreme authority, the Marine Superintendent, the Harbour-Master—a very great person in the eyes of every single quill-driver*in the room. But that was nothing to the opinion he had of his own greatness.

Captain Ellis looked upon himself as a sort of divine

(pagan) emanation, the deputy-Neptune for the cir-
cumambient seas. If he did not actually rule the
waves, he pretended to rule the fate of the mortals whose
lives were cast upon the waters.

This uplifting illusion made him inquisitorial and
peremptory. And as his temperament was chóleric
there were fellows who were actually afraid of him. He
was redoubtable, not in virtue of his office, but because
of his unwarrantable assumptions. I had never had
anything to do with him before.

I said: "Oh! He has asked for me twice. Then
perhaps I had better go in."

"You must! You must!"

The shipping-master led the way with a mincing gait
round the whole system of desks to a tall and important-
looking door, which he opened with a deferential action
of the arm.

He stepped right in (but without letting go of the
handle) and, after gazing reverently down the room for
a while, beckoned me in by a silent jerk of the head.
Then he slipped out at once and shut the door after me
most delicately.

Three lofty windows gave on the harbour. There
was nothing in them but the dark-blue sparkling sea and
the paler luminous blue of the sky. My eye caught in
the depths and distances of these blue tones the white
speck of some big ship just arrived and about to anchor
in the outer roadstead.* A ship from home—after
perhaps ninety days at sea. There is something
touching about a ship coming in from sea and folding
her white wings for a rest.

The next thing I saw was the top-knot of silver hair
surmounting Captain Ellis' smooth red face, which
would have been apoplectic if it hadn't had such a fresh
appearance.

Our deputy-Neptune* had no beard on his chin, and there was no trident to be seen standing in a corner anywhere, like an umbrella. But his hand was holding a pen—the official pen, far mightier than the sword*in making or marring the fortune of simple toiling men. He was looking over his shoulder at my advance.

When I had come well within range he saluted me by a nerve-shattering: "Where have you been all this time?"

As it was no concern of his I did not take the slightest notice of the shot. I said simply that I had heard there was a master needed for some vessel, and being a sailing-ship man I thought I would apply. . . .

He interrupted me. "Why! Hang it! *You* are the right man for that job—if there had been twenty others after it. But no fear of that. They are all afraid to catch hold. That's what's the matter."

He was very irritated. I said innocently: "Are they sir? I wonder why?"

"Why!" he fumed. "Afraid of the sails. Afraid of a white crew. Too much trouble. Too much work. Too long out here. Easy life and deck-chairs more their mark. Here I sit with the Consul-General's*cable before me, and the only man fit for the job not to be found anywhere. I began to think you were funking it too. . . ."

"I haven't been long getting to the office," I remarked calmly.

"You have a good name out here, though," he growled savagely without looking at me.

"I am very glad to hear it from you, sir," I said.

"Yes. But you are not on the spot when you are wanted. You know you weren't. That steward of yours wouldn't dare to neglect a message from this office. Where the devil did you hide yourself for the best part of the day?"

I only smiled kindly down on him, and he seemed to recollect himself, and asked me to take a seat. He explained that the master of a British ship having died in Bankok* the Consul-General had cabled to him a request for a competent man to be sent out to take command.

Apparently, in his mind, I was the man from the first, though for the looks of the thing the notification addressed to the Sailors' Home was general. An agreement had already been prepared. He gave it to me to read, and when I handed it back to him with the remark that I accepted its terms, the deputy-Neptune signed it, stamped it with his own exalted hand, folded it in four (it was a sheet of blue foolscap), and presented it to me— a gift of extraordinary potency, for, as I put it in my pocket, my head swam a little.

"This is your appointment to the command," he said with a certain gravity. "An official appointment binding the owners to conditions which you have accepted. Now—when will you be ready to go?"

I said I would be ready that very day if necessary. He caught me at my word with great readiness. The steamer *Melita* was leaving for Bankok that evening about seven. He would request her captain officially to give me a passage and wait for me till ten o'clock.

Then he rose from his office chair, and I got up too. My head swam, there was no doubt about it, and I felt a heaviness of limbs as if they had grown bigger since I had sat down on that chair. I made my bow.

A subtle change in Captain Ellis' manner became perceptible as though he had laid aside the trident of deputy-Neptune. In reality, it was only his official pen that he had dropped on getting up.*

II

He shook hands with me: "Well, there you are, on your own, appointed officially under my responsibility."

He was actually walking with me to the door. What a distance off it seemed! I moved like a man in bonds. But we reached it at last. I opened it with the sensation of dealing with mere dream-stuff, and then at the last moment the fellowship of seamen asserted itself, stronger than the difference of age and station. It asserted itself in Captain Ellis' voice.

"Good-bye—and good luck to you," he said so heartily that I could only give him a grateful glance. Then I turned and went out, never to see him again in my life. I had not made three steps into the outer office when I heard behind my back a gruff, loud, authoritative voice, the voice of our deputy-Neptune.

It was addressing the head shipping-master, who, having let me in, had, apparently, remained hovering in the middle distance ever since.

"Mr. R., let the harbour launch have steam up to take the captain here on board the *Melita* at half-past nine to-night."

I was amazed at the startled assent of R.'s "Yes, sir." He ran before me out on the landing. My new dignity sat yet so lightly on me that I was not aware that it was I, the Captain, the object of this last graciousness. It seemed as if all of a sudden a pair of wings had grown on my shoulders. I merely skimmed along the polished floor.

But R. was impressed.

"I say!" he exclaimed on the landing, while the
Malay crew of the steam-launch standing by looked
stonily at the man for whom they were going to be
kept on duty so late, away from their gambling, from
their girls, or their pure domestic joys. "I say! His
own launch. What have you done to him?"

His stare was full of respectful curiosity. I was quite
confounded.

"Was it for me? I hadn't the slightest notion,"
I stammered out.

He nodded many times. "Yes. And the last person
who had it before you was a Duke. So, there!"

I think he expected me to faint on the spot. But I
was in too much of a hurry for emotional displays. My
feelings were already in such a whirl that this staggering
information did not seem to make the slightest difference. It fell into the seething cauldron of my brain, and
I carried it off with me after a short but effusive passage
of leave-taking with R.

The favour of the great throws an aureole*round the
fortunate object of its selection. That excellent man
inquired whether he could do anything for me. He had
known me only by sight, and he was well aware he
would never see me again; I was, in common with the
other seamen of the port, merely a subject for official
writing, filling up of forms with all the artificial superior-
ity of a man of pen and ink*to the men who grapple with
realities outside the consecrated walls of official build-
ings. What ghosts we must have been to him! Mere
symbols to juggle with in books and heavy registers,
without brains and muscles and perplexities; something
hardly useful and decidedly inferior.

And he—the office hours being over—wanted to know
if he could be of any use to me!

I ought, properly speaking—I ought to have been

moved to tears. But I did not even think of it. It was
only another miraculous manifestation of that day of
miracles. I parted from him as if he had been a mere
symbol. I floated down the staircase. I floated out of
the official and imposing portal. I went on floating
along.

I use that word rather than the word "flew," because
I have a distinct impression that, though uplifted by my
aroused youth, my movements were deliberate enough.
To that mixed white, brown, and yellow portion of
mankind, out abroad on their own affairs, I presented
the appearance of a man walking rather sedately. And
nothing in the way of abstraction could have equalled
my deep detachment from the forms and colours of this
world. It was, as it were, absolute.

And yet, suddenly, I recognised Hamilton. I recognised him without effort, without a shock, without a
start. There he was, strolling towards the Harbour
Office with his stiff, arrogant dignity. His red face
made him noticeable at a distance. It flamed, over
there, on the shady side of the street.

He had perceived me too. Something (unconscious
exuberance of spirits perhaps) moved me to wave my
hand to him elaborately. This lapse from good taste
happened before I was aware that I was capable of it.

The impact of my impudence stopped him short,
much as a bullet might have done. I verily believe he
staggered, though as far as I could see he didn't actually
fall. I had gone past in a moment and did not turn my
head. I had forgotten his existence.

The next ten minutes might have been ten seconds or
ten centuries for all my consciousness had to do with it.
People might have been falling dead around me, houses
crumbling, guns firing, I wouldn't have known. I was
thinking: "By Jove! I have got it." *It* being the

command. It had come about in a way utterly unforeseen in my modest day-dreams.

I perceived that my imagination had been running in conventional channels and that my hopes had always been drab stuff. I had envisaged a command as a result of a slow course of promotion in the employ of some highly respectable firm. The reward of faithful service. Well, faithful service was all right. One would naturally give that for one's own sake, for the sake of the ship, for the love of the life of one's choice; not for the sake of the reward.

There is something distasteful in the notion of a reward.

And now here I had my command, absolutely in my pocket, in a way undeniable indeed, but most unexpected; beyond my imaginings, outside all reasonable expectations, and even notwithstanding the existence of some sort of obscure intrigue to keep it away from me. It is true that the intrigue was feeble, but it helped the feeling of wonder—as if I had been specially destined for that ship I did not know, by some power higher than the prosaic agencies of the commercial world.

A strange sense of exultation began to creep into me. If I had worked for that command ten years or more there would have been nothing of the kind. I was a little frightened.

"Let us be calm," I said to myself.

Outside the door of the Officers' Home the wretched Steward seemed to be waiting for me. There was a broad flight of a few steps, and he ran to and fro on the top of it as if chained there. A distressed cur. He looked as though his throat were too dry for him to bark.

I regret to say I stopped before going in. There had been a revolution in my moral nature. He waited open-mouthed, breathless, while I looked at him for half a minute.

"And you thought you could keep me out of it," I said scathingly.

"You said you were going home," he squeaked miserably. "You said so. You said so."

"I wonder what Captain Ellis will have to say to that excuse," I uttered slowly with a sinister meaning.

His lower jaw had been trembling all the time and his voice was like the bleating of a sick goat. "You have given me away? You have done for me?"

Neither his distress nor yet the sheer absurdity of it was able to disarm me. It was the first instance of harm being attempted to be done to me—at any rate, the first I had ever found out. And I was still young enough, still too much on this side of the shadow-line, not to be surprised*and indignant at such things.

I gazed at him inflexibly. Let the beggar suffer. He slapped his forehead and I passed in, pursued, into the dining-room, by his screech: "I always said you'd be the death of me."

This clamour not only overtook me, but went ahead as it were on to the verandah and brought out Captain Giles.

He stood before me in the doorway in all the commonplace solidity of his wisdom. The gold chain glittered on his breast. He clutched a smouldering pipe.

I extended my hand to him warmly and he seemed surprised, but did respond heartily enough in the end, with a faint smile of superior knowledge which cut my thanks short as if with a knife. I don't think that more than one word came out. And even for that one, judging by the temperature of my face, I had blushed as if for a bad action. Assuming a detached tone, I wondered how on earth he had managed to spot the little underhand game that had been going on.

He murmured complacently that there were but few things done in the town that he could not see the inside of. And as to this house, he had been using it off and on for nearly ten years. Nothing that went on in it could escape his great experience. It had been no trouble to him. No trouble at all.

Then in his quiet thick tone he wanted to know if I had complained formally of the Steward's action.

I said that I hadn't—though, indeed, it was not for want of opportunity. Captain Ellis had gone for me bald-headed in a most ridiculous fashion for being out of the way when wanted.

"Funny old gentleman," interjected Captain Giles. "What did you say to that?"

"I said simply that I came along the very moment I heard of his message. Nothing more. I didn't want to hurt the Steward. I would scorn to harm such an object. No. I made no complaint, but I believe he thinks I've done so. Let him think. He's got a fright that he won't forget in a hurry, for Captain Ellis would kick him out into the middle of Asia. . . ."

"Wait a moment," said Captain Giles, leaving me suddenly. I sat down feeling very tired, mostly in my head. Before I could start a train of thought he stood again before me, murmuring the excuse that he had to go and put the fellow's mind at ease.

I looked up with surprise. But in reality I was indifferent. He explained that he had found the Steward lying face downwards on the horsehair sofa. He was all right now.

"He would not have died of fright," I said contemptuously.

"No. But he might have taken an overdose out of

one of those little bottles he keeps in his room," Captain Giles argued seriously. "The confounded fool has tried to poison himself once—a couple of years ago."

"Really," I said without emotion. "He doesn't seem very fit to live, anyhow."

"As to that, it may be said of a good many."

"Don't exaggerate like this!" I protested, laughing irritably. "But I wonder what this part of the world would do if you were to leave off looking after it, Captain Giles? Here you have got me a command and saved the Steward's life in one afternoon. Though why you should have taken all that interest in either of us is more than I can understand."

Captain Giles remained silent for a minute.

Then gravely:

"He's not a bad steward really. He can find a good cook, at any rate. And, what's more, he can keep him when found. I remember the cooks we had here before his time. . . ."

I must have made a movement of impatience, because he interrupted himself with an apology for keeping me yarning there, while no doubt I needed all my time to get ready.

What I really needed was to be alone for a bit. I seized this opening hastily. My bedroom was a quiet refuge in an apparently uninhabited wing of the building. Having absolutely nothing to do (for I had not unpacked my things), I sat down on the bed and abandoned myself to the influences of the hour. To the unexpected influences. . . .

And first I wondered at my state of mind. Why was I not more surprised? Why? Here I was, invested with a command in the twinkling of an eye, not in the common course of human affairs, but more as if by enchantment. I ought to have been lost in aston-

ishment. But I wasn't. I was very much like people
in fairy tales. Nothing ever astonishes them. When
a fully appointed gala coach is produced out of a pump-
kin to take her to a ball Cinderella does not exclaim.
She gets in quietly and drives away to her high fortune.

Captain Ellis (a fierce sort of fairy) had produced a
command out of a drawer almost as unexpectedly as in
a fairy tale. But a command is an abstract idea, and it
seemed a sort of "lesser marvel" till it flashed upon me
that it involved the concrete existence of a ship.

A ship! My ship! She was mine, more absolutely
mine for possession and care than anything in the
world; an object of responsibility and devotion. She
was there waiting for me, spellbound, unable to move,
to live, to get out into the world (till I came), like
an enchanted princess. Her call had come to me as
if from the clouds. I had never suspected her existence.
I didn't know how she looked, I had barely heard her
name, and yet we were indissolubly united for a certain
portion of our future, to sink or swim together!

A sudden passion of anxious impatience rushed
through my veins and gave me such a sense of the
intensity of existence as I have never felt before or since.
I discovered how much of a seaman I was, in heart, in
mind, and, as it were, physically—a man exclusively of
sea and ships; the sea the only world that counted, and
the ships the test of manliness, of temperament, of
courage and fidelity—and of love.

I had an exquisite moment. It was unique also.
Jumping up from my seat, I paced up and down my
room for a long time. But when I came into the dining-
room I behaved with sufficient composure. I only
couldn't eat anything at dinner.

Having declared my intention not to drive but to
walk down to the quay, I must render the wretched

Steward justice that he bestirred himself to find me some coolies*for the luggage. They departed, carrying all my worldly possessions (except a little money I had in my pocket) slung from a long pole. Captain Giles volunteered to walk down with me.

We followed the sombre, shaded alley across the Esplanade. It was moderately cool there under the trees. Captain Giles remarked, with a sudden laugh: "I know who's jolly thankful at having seen the last of you."

I guess that he meant the Steward. The fellow had borne himself to me in a sulkily frightened manner at the last. I expressed my wonder that he should have tried to do me a bad turn for no reason at all.

"Don't you see that what he wanted was to get rid of our friend Hamilton by dodging him in front of you for that job? That would have removed him for good, see?"

"Heavens!" I exclaimed, feeling humiliated somehow. "Can it be possible? What a fool he must be! That overbearing, impudent loafer! Why! He couldn't . . . And yet he's nearly done it, I believe; for the Harbour Office was bound to send somebody."

"Aye. A fool like our Steward can be dangerous sometimes," declared Captain Giles sententiously. "Just because he is a fool," he added, imparting further instruction in his complacent low tones. "For," he continued in the manner of a set demonstration, "no sensible person would risk being kicked out of the only berth between himself and starvation just to get rid of a simple annoyance—a small worry. Would he now?"

"Well, no," I conceded, restraining a desire to laugh at that something mysteriously earnest in delivering the conclusions of his wisdom as though they were the product of prohibited operations. "But that fellow looks as if he were rather crazy. He must be."

"As to that, I believe everybody in the world is a little mad," he announced quietly.*

"You make no exceptions?" I inquired, just to hear his answer.

He kept silent for a little while, then got home in an effective manner.

"Why! Kent says that even of you."

"Does he?" I retorted, extremely embittered all at once against my former captain. "There's nothing of that in the written character from him which I've got in my pocket. Has he given you any instances of my lunacy?"

Captain Giles explained in a conciliating tone that it had been only a friendly remark in reference to my abrupt leaving the ship for no apparent reason.

I muttered grumpily: "Oh! leaving his ship," and mended my pace. He kept up by my side in the deep gloom of the avenue as if it were his conscientious duty to see me out of the colony as an undesirable character. He panted a little, which was rather pathetic in a way. But I was not moved. On the contrary. His discomfort gave me a sort of malicious pleasure.

Presently I relented, slowed down, and said:

"What I really wanted was to get a fresh grip. I felt it was time. Is that so very mad?"

He made no answer. We were issuing from the avenue. On the bridge over the canal a dark, irresolute figure seemed to be awaiting something or somebody.

It was a Malay policeman, barefooted, in his blue uniform. The silver band on his little round cap shone dimly in the light of the street lamp. He peered in our direction timidly.

Before we could come up to him he turned about and

walked in front of us in the direction of the jetty. The distance was some hundred yards; and then I found my coolies squatting on their heels. They had kept the pole on their shoulders, and all my worldly goods, still tied to the pole, were resting on the ground between them. As far as the eye could reach along the quay there was not another soul abroad except the police peon, who saluted us.

It seems he had detained the coolies as suspicious characters, and had forbidden them the jetty. But at a sign from me he took off the embargo with alacrity. The two patient fellows, rising together with a faint grunt, trotted off along the planks, and I prepared to take my leave of Captain Giles, who stood there with an air as though his mission were drawing to a close. It could not be denied that he had done it all. And while I hesitated about an appropriate sentence he made himself heard:

"I expect you'll have your hands pretty full of tangled up business."

I asked him what made him think so; and he answered that it was his general experience of the world. Ship a long time away from her port, owners inaccessible by cable, and the only man who could explain matters dead and buried.

"And you yourself new to the business in a way," he concluded in a sort of unanswerable tone.

"Don't insist," I said. "I know it only too well. I only wish you could impart to me some small portion of your experience before I go. As it can't be done in ten minutes I had better not begin to ask you. There's that harbour-launch waiting for me too. But I won't feel really at peace till I have that ship of mine out in the Indian Ocean."

He remarked casually that from Bankok to the

Indian Ocean was a pretty long step. And this murmur, like a dim flash from a dark lantern, showed me for a moment the broad belt of islands and reefs between that unknown ship, which was mine, and the freedom of the great waters of the globe.

But I felt no apprehension. I was familiar enough with the Archipelago by that time. Extreme patience and extreme care would see me through the region of broken land, of faint airs and of dead water to where I would feel at last my command swing on the great swell and list over to the great breath of regular winds, that would give her the feeling of a large, more intense life. The road would be long. All roads are long that lead towards one's heart's desire. But this road my mind's eye could see on a chart, professionally, with all its complications and difficulties, yet simple enough in a way. One is a seaman or one is not. And I had no doubt of being one.

The only part I was a stranger to was the Gulf of Siam. And I mentioned this to Captain Giles. Not that I was concerned very much. It belonged to the same region the nature of which I knew, into whose very soul I seemed to have looked during the last months of that existence with which I had broken now, suddenly, as one parts with some enchanting company.

"The Gulf . . . Ay! A funny piece of water—that," said Captain Giles.

Funny, in this connection, was a vague word. The whole thing sounded like an opinion uttered by a cautious person mindful of actions for slander.

I didn't inquire as to the nature of that funniness. There was really no time. But at the very last he volunteered a warning.

"Whatever you do keep to the east side of it. The

west side is dangerous at this time of the year. Don't let anything tempt you over. You'll find nothing but trouble there."

Though I could hardly imagine what could tempt me to involve my ship amongst the currents and reefs of the Malay shore, I thanked him for the advice.

He gripped my extended arm warmly, and the end of our acquaintance came suddenly in the words: "Good-night."

That was all he said: "Good-night." Nothing more. I don't know what I intended to say, but surprise made me swallow it, whatever it was. I choked slightly, and then exclaimed with a sort of nervous haste: "Oh! Good-night, Captain Giles, good-night."

His movements were always deliberate, but his back had receded some distance along the deserted quay before I collected myself enough to follow his example and made a half turn in the direction of the jetty.

Only my movements were not deliberate. I hurried down to the steps and leaped into the launch. Before I had fairly landed in her stern-sheets*the slim little craft darted away from the jetty with a sudden swirl of her propeller and the hard, rapid puffing of the exhaust in her vaguely gleaming brass funnel amidships.

The misty churning at her stern was the only sound in the world. The shore lay plunged in the silence of the deepest slumber.* I watched the town recede still and soundless in the hot night, till the abrupt hail, "Steam-launch, ahoy!" made me spin round face forward. We were close to a white, ghostly steamer. Lights shone on her decks, in her portholes. And the same voice shouted from her: "Is that our passenger?"

"It is," I yelled.

Her crew had been obviously on the jump. I could hear them running about. The modern spirit of haste was loudly vocal in the orders to "Heave away on the cable"—to "Lower the side-ladder," and in urgent requests to me to "Come along, sir! We have been delayed three hours for you. . . . Our time is seven o'clock, you know!"

I stepped on the deck. I said "No! I don't know." The spirit of modern hurry was embodied in a thin, long-armed, long-legged man, with a closely clipped grey beard. His meagre hand was hot and dry. He declared feverishly:

"I am hanged if I would have waited another five minutes—harbour-master or no harbour-master."

"That's your own business," I said. "I didn't ask you to wait for me."

"I hope you don't expect any supper," he burst out. "This isn't a boarding-house afloat. You are the first passenger I ever had in my life and I hope to goodness you will be the last."

I made no answer to this hospitable communication; and, indeed, he didn't wait for any, bolting away on to his bridge to get his ship under way.

For the four days he had me on board he did not depart from that half-hostile attitude. His ship having been delayed three hours on my account he couldn't forgive me for not being a more distinguished person. He was not exactly outspoken about it, but that feeling of annoyed wonder was peeping out perpetually in his talk.

He was absurd.

He was also a man of much experience, which he liked to trot out; but no greater contrast with Captain Giles could have been imagined. He would have amused me if I had wanted to be amused. But I did not want to be amused. I was like a lover looking forward to a meeting. Human hostility was nothing to me. I thought of my unknown ship. It was amusement enough, torment enough, occupation enough.

He perceived my state, for his wits were sufficiently sharp for that, and he poked sly fun at my preoccupation in the manner some nasty, cynical old men assume towards the dreams and illusions of youth. I, on my side, refrained from questioning him as to the appearance of my ship, though I knew that being in Bankok every month or so he must have known her by sight. I was not going to expose the ship, my ship! to some slighting reference.

He was the first really unsympathetic man I had ever come in contact with. My education was far from being finished, though I didn't know it. No! I didn't know it.

All I knew was that he disliked me and had some contempt for my person. Why? Apparently because his ship had been delayed three hours on my account. Who was I to have such a thing done for me? Such a thing had never been done for him. It was a sort of jealous indignation.

My expectation, mingled with fear, was wrought to its highest pitch. How slow had been the days of the passage and how soon they were over. One morning early, we crossed the bar,* and while the sun was rising splendidly over the flat spaces of the land we steamed up the innumerable bends, passed under the shadow of the great gilt pagoda, and reached the outskirts of the town.

There it was, spread largely on both banks, the Oriental capital* which had as yet suffered no white conqueror; an expanse of brown houses of bamboo, of mats, of leaves, of a vegetable-matter style of architecture, sprung out of the brown soil on the banks of the muddy river. It was amazing to think that in those miles of human habitations there was not probably half a dozen pounds of nails. Some of those houses of sticks and grass, like the nests of an aquatic race, clung to the low shores. Others seemed to grow out of the water; others again floated in long anchored rows in the very middle of the stream. Here and there in the distance, above the crowded mob of low, brown roof ridges, towered great piles of masonry, King's Palace, temples, gorgeous and dilapidated, crumbling under the vertical sunlight, tremendous, overpowering, almost palpable, which seemed to enter one's breast with the breath of one's nostrils and soak into one's limbs through every pore of one's skin.

The ridiculous victim of jealousy had for some reason or other to stop his engines just then. The steamer drifted slowly up with the tide. Oblivious of my new surroundings I walked the deck, in anxious, deadened abstraction, a commingling of romantic reverie with a very practical survey of my qualifications. For the time was approaching for me to behold my command and to prove my worth in the ultimate test of my profession.

Suddenly I heard myself called by that imbecile. He was beckoning me to come up on his bridge.

I didn't care very much for that, but as it seemed that he had something particular to say I went up the ladder.

He laid his hand on my shoulder and gave me a slight turn, pointing with his other arm at the same time.

"There! That's your ship, Captain," he said. I felt a thump in my breast—only one, as if my heart had ceased to beat. There were ten or more ships moored along the bank, and the one he meant was partly hidden from my sight by her next astern. He said: "We'll drift abreast her in a moment."

What was his tone? Mocking? Threatening? Or only indifferent? I could not tell. I suspected some malice in this unexpected manifestation of interest.

He left me, and I leaned over the rail of the bridge looking over the side. I dared not raise my eyes. Yet it had to be done—and, indeed, I could not have helped myself. I believe I trembled.

But directly my eyes had rested on my ship all my fear vanished. It went off swiftly, like a bad dream. Only that a dream leaves no shame behind it, and that I felt a momentary shame at my unworthy suspicions.

Yes, there she was.* Her hull, her rigging filled my eye with a great content. That feeling of life-emptiness which had made me so restless for the last few months lost its bitter plausibility, its evil influence, dissolved in a flow of joyous emotion.

At the first glance I saw that she was a high-class vessel, a harmonious creature in the lines of her fine body, in the proportioned tallness of her spars. Whatever her age and her history, she had preserved the stamp of her origin. She was one of those craft that in virtue of their design and complete finish will never look old. Amongst her companions moored to the bank, and all bigger than herself, she looked like a creature of high breed—an Arab steed in a string of cart-horses.

A voice behind me said in a nasty equivocal tone: "I hope you are satisfied with her, Captain." I did not even turn my head. It was the master of the steamer, and whatever he meant, whatever he thought of her, I knew that, like some rare women, she was one of those creatures whose mere existence is enough to awaken an unselfish delight. One feels that it is good to be in the world in which she has her being.

That illusion of life and character which charms one

in men's finest handiwork radiated from her. An enormous baulk* of teak-wood timber swung over her hatchway; lifeless matter, looking heavier and bigger than anything aboard of her. When they started lowering it the surge of the tackle sent a quiver through her from water-line to the trucks up the fine nerves of her rigging, as though she had shuddered at the weight. It seemed cruel to load her so. . . .

Half-an-hour later, putting my foot on her deck for the first time, I received the feeling of deep physical satisfaction. Nothing could equal the fullness of that moment, the ideal completeness of that emotional experience which had come to me without the preliminary toil and disenchantments of an obscure career.

My rapid glance ran over her, enveloped, appropriated the form concreting the abstract sentiment of my command. A lot of details perceptible to a seaman struck my eye vividly in that instant. For the rest, I saw her disengaged from the material conditions of her being. The shore to which she was moored was as if it did not exist. What were to me all the countries of the globe? In all the parts of the world washed by navigable waters our relation to each other would be the same—and more intimate than there are words to express in the language. Apart from that, every scene and episode would be a mere passing show. The very gang of yellow coolies busy about the main hatch was less substantial than the stuff dreams are made of. For who on earth would dream of Chinamen? . . .

I went aft, ascended the poop, where, under the awning,* gleamed the brasses of the yacht-like fittings, the polished surfaces of the rails, the glass of the skylights. Right aft two seamen, busy cleaning the steering gear, with the reflected ripples of light running playfully up their bent backs, went on with their work,

unaware of me and of the almost affectionate glance I
threw at them in passing towards the companion-way*of
the cabin.

The doors stood wide open, the slide was pushed
right back. The half-turn of the staircase cut off the
view of the lobby.* A low humming ascended from
below, but it stopped abruptly at the sound of my
descending footsteps.

III

THE first thing I saw down there was the upper part of a man's body projecting backwards, as it were, from one of the doors at the foot of the stairs. His eyes looked at me very wide and still. In one hand he held a dinner plate, in the other a cloth.

"I am your new captain," I said quietly.

In a moment, in the twinkling of an eye, he had got rid of the plate and the cloth and jumped to open the cabin door. As soon as I passed into the saloon he vanished, but only to reappear instantly, buttoning up a jacket he had put on with the swiftness of a "quick-change" artist.

"Where's the chief mate?" I asked.

"In the hold, I think, sir. I saw him go down the after-hatch ten minutes ago."

"Tell him I am on board."

The mahogany table under the skylight shone in the twilight like a dark pool of water. The sideboard, surmounted by a wide looking-glass in an ormolu*frame, had a marble top. It bore a pair of silver-plated lamps and some other pieces—obviously a harbour display. The saloon itself was panelled in two kinds of wood in the excellent, simple taste prevailing when the ship was built.

I sat down in the arm-chair at the head of the table— the captain's chair, with a small tell-tale compass swung above it—a mute reminder of unremitting vigilance.

A succession of men had sat in that chair. I became

aware of that thought suddenly, vividly, as though
each had left a little of himself between the four walls of
these ornate bulkheads;*as if a sort of composite soul,
the soul of command, had whispered suddenly to mine
of long days at sea and of anxious moments.

"You, too!" it seemed to say, "you, too, shall taste
of that peace and that unrest in a searching intimacy
with your own self—obscure as we were and as supreme
in the face of all the winds and all the seas, in an immensity that receives no impress, preserves no memories, and keeps no reckoning of lives."

Deep within the tarnished ormolu frame, in the hot
half-light sifted through the awning, I saw my own
face propped between my hands. And I stared back at
myself with the perfect detachment of distance, rather
with curiosity than with any other feeling, except of
some sympathy for this latest representative of what
for all intents and purposes was a dynasty; continuous
not in blood, indeed, but in its experience, in its training, in its conception of duty, and in the blessed simplicity of its traditional point of view on life.

It struck me that this quietly staring man whom I
was watching, both as if he were myself and somebody
else, was not exactly a lonely figure. He had his place
in a line of men whom he did not know, of whom he had
never heard; but who were fashioned by the same influences, whose souls in relation to their humble life's
work had no secrets for him.

Suddenly I perceived that there was another man in
the saloon, standing a little on one side and looking
intently at me. The chief mate. His long, red
moustache determined the character of his physiognomy, which struck me as pugnacious in (strange to
say) a ghastly sort of way.

How long had he been there looking at me, appraising

me in my unguarded day-dreaming state? I would have been more disconcerted if, having the clock set in the top of the mirror-frame right in front of me, I had not noticed that its long hand had hardly moved at all.

I could not have been in that cabin more than two minutes altogether. Say three. . . . So he could not have been watching me more than a mere fraction of a minute, luckily. Still, I regretted the occurrence.

But I showed nothing of it as I rose leisurely (it had to be leisurely) and greeted him with perfect friendliness.

There was something reluctant and at the same time attentive in his bearing. His name was Burns. We left the cabin and went round the ship together. His face in the full light of day appeared very worn, meagre, even haggard. Somehow I had a delicacy as to looking too often at him; his eyes, on the contrary, remained fairly glued on my face. They were greenish and had an expectant expression.

He answered all my questions readily enough, but my ear seemed to catch a tone of unwillingness. The second officer, with three or four hands, was busy forward. The mate mentioned his name and I nodded to him in passing. He was very young. He struck me as rather a cub.

When we returned below I sat down on one end of a deep, semi-circular, or, rather, semi-oval settee, upholstered in red plush. It extended right across the whole after-end of the cabin. Mr. Burns, motioned to sit down, dropped into one of the swivel-chairs round the table, and kept his eyes on me as persistently as ever, and with that strange air as if all this were make-believe and he expected me to get up, burst into a laugh, slap him on the back, and vanish from the cabin.

There was an odd stress in the situation which began

to make me uncomfortable. I tried to react against this vague feeling.

"It's only my inexperience," I thought.

In the face of that man, several years, I judged, older than myself, I became aware of what I had left already behind me—my youth. And that was indeed poor comfort. Youth is a fine thing, a mighty power—as long as one does not think of it. I felt I was becoming self-conscious. Almost against my will I assumed a moody gravity. I said: "I see you have kept her in very good order, Mr. Burns."

Directly I had uttered these words I asked myself angrily why the deuce did I want to say that? Mr. Burns in answer had only blinked at me. What on earth did he mean?

I fell back on a question which had been in my thoughts for a long time—the most natural question on the lips of any seaman whatever joining a ship. I voiced it (confound this self-consciousness) in a *dégagé**cheerful tone: "I suppose she can travel—what?"*

Now a question like this might have been answered normally, either in accents of apologetic sorrow or with a visibly suppressed pride, in a "I don't want to boast, but you shall see" sort of tone. There are sailors, too, who would have been roughly outspoken: "Lazy brute," or openly delighted: "She's a flyer." Two ways, if four manners.

But Mr. Burns found another way, a way of his own which had, at all events, the merit of saving his breath, if no other.

Again he did not say anything. He only frowned. And it was an angry frown. I waited. Nothing more came.

"What's the matter? . . . Can't you tell after

being nearly two years in the ship?" I addressed him sharply.

He looked as startled for a moment as though he had discovered my presence only that very moment. But this passed off almost at once. He put on an air of indifference. But I suppose he thought it better to say something. He said that a ship needed, just like a man, the chance to show the best she could do, and that this ship had never had a chance since he had been on board of her. Not that he could remember. The last captain . . . He paused.

"Has he been so very unlucky?" I asked with frank incredulity. Mr. Burns turned his eyes away from me. No, the late captain was not an unlucky man. One couldn't say that. But he had not seemed to want to make use of his luck.

Mr. Burns—man of enigmatic moods—made this statement with an inanimate face and staring wilfully at the rudder-casing. The statement itself was obscurely suggestive. I asked quietly:

"Where did he die?"

"In this saloon. Just where you are sitting now," answered Mr. Burns.

I repressed a silly impulse to jump up; but upon the whole I was relieved to hear that he had not died in the bed which was now to be mine. I pointed out to the chief mate that what I really wanted to know was where he had buried his late captain.

Mr. Burns said that it was at the entrance to the Gulf. A roomy grave; a sufficient answer. But the mate, overcoming visibly something within him—something like a curious reluctance to believe in my advent (as an irrevocable fact, at any rate), did not stop at that—though, indeed, he may have wished to do so.

As a compromise with his feelings, I believe, he addressed himself persistently to the rudder-casing, so that to me he had the appearance of a man talking in solitude, a little unconsciously, however.

His tale was that at seven bells in the forenoon watch* he had all hands mustered on the quarter-deck and told them that they had better go down to say good-bye to the captain.

Those words, as if grudged to an intruding personage, were enough for me to evoke vividly that strange ceremony: The bare-footed, bare-headed seamen crowding shyly into that cabin, a small mob pressed against that sideboard, uncomfortable rather than moved, shirts open on sunburnt chests, weather-beaten faces, and all staring at the dying man with the same grave and expectant expression.

"Was he conscious?" I asked.

"He didn't speak, but he moved his eyes to look at them," said the mate.

After waiting a moment Mr. Burns motioned the crew to leave the cabin, but he detained the two eldest men to stay with the captain while he went on deck with his sextant to "take the sun." It was getting towards noon and he was anxious to obtain a good observation for latitude. When he returned below to put his sextant away he found that the two men had retreated out into the lobby. Through the open door he had a view of the captain lying easy against the pillows. He had "passed away" while Mr. Burns was taking his observation. As near noon as possible. He had hardly changed his position.

Mr. Burns sighed, glanced at me inquisitively, as much as to say, "Aren't you going yet?" and then turned his thoughts from his new captain back to the old, who, being dead, had no authority, was not in anybody's way, and was much easier to deal with.

Mr. Burns dealt with him at some length. He was a
peculiar man—of about sixty-five—iron grey, hard-
faced, obstinate, and uncommunicative. He used to
keep the ship loafing at sea for inscrutable reasons.
Would come on deck at night sometimes, take some sail
off her, God only knows why or wherefore, then go below, shut himself up in his cabin, and play on the violin
for hours—till daybreak perhaps. In fact, he spent
most of his time day or night playing the violin. That
was when the fit took him. Very loud, too.

It came to this, that Mr. Burns mustered his
courage one day and remonstrated earnestly with the
captain. Neither he nor the second mate could get a
wink of sleep in their watches below for the noise. . . .
And how could they be expected to keep awake while
on duty? he pleaded. The answer of that stern man
was that if he and the second mate didn't like the noise,
they were welcome to pack up their traps*and walk
over the side. When this alternative was offered the
ship happened to be 600 miles from the nearest land.

Mr. Burns at this point looked at me with an air of
curiosity. I began to think that my predecessor was a
remarkably peculiar old man.

But I had to hear stranger things yet. It came out
that this stern, grim, wind-tanned, rough, sea-salted,
taciturn sailor of sixty-five was not only an artist, but
a lover as well. In Haiphong,*when they got there
after a course of most unprofitable peregrinations
(during which the ship was nearly lost twice), he got
himself, in Mr. Burns' own words, "mixed up" with
some woman. Mr. Burns had had no personal knowledge of that affair, but positive evidence of it existed
in the shape of a photograph taken in Haiphong. Mr.
Burns found it in one of the drawers in the captain's
room.

In due course I, too, saw that amazing human document (I even threw it overboard later). There he sat with his hands reposing on his knees, bald, squat, grey, bristly, recalling a wild boar somehow; and by his side towered an awful, mature, white female with rapacious nostrils and a cheaply ill-omened stare in her enormous eyes. She was disguised in some semi-oriental, vulgar, fancy costume. She resembled a low-class medium or one of those women who tell fortunes by cards for half-a-crown.* And yet she was striking. A professional sorceress from the slums. It was incomprehensible. There was something awful in the thought that she was the last reflection of the world of passion for the fierce soul which seemed to look at one out of the sardonically savage face of that old seaman. However, I noticed that she was holding some musical instrument— guitar or mandoline—in her hand. Perhaps that was the secret of her sortilege.*

For Mr. Burns that photograph explained why the unloaded ship was kept sweltering at anchor for three weeks in a pestilential hot harbour without air. They lay there and gasped. The captain, appearing now and then on short visits, mumbled to Mr. Burns unlikely tales about some letters he was waiting for.

Suddenly, after vanishing for a week, he came on board in the middle of the night and took the ship out to sea with the first break of dawn. Daylight showed him looking wild and ill. The mere getting clear of the land took two days, and somehow or other they bumped slightly on a reef. However, no leak developed, and the captain, growling "no matter," informed Mr. Burns that he had made up his mind to take the ship to Hong-Kong and dry-dock her there.

At this Mr. Burns was plunged into despair. For indeed, to beat up to Hong-Kong against a fierce monsoon, with a ship not sufficiently ballasted and with her supply of water not completed, was an insane project.

But the captain growled peremptorily, "Stick her at it," and Mr. Burns, dismayed and enraged, stuck her at it, and kept her at it, blowing away sails, straining the spars, exhausting the crew—nearly maddened by the absolute conviction that the attempt was impossible and was bound to end in some catastrophe.

Meantime the captain, shut up in his cabin and wedged in a corner of his settee against the crazy bounding of the ship, played the violin—or, at any rate, made continuous noise on it.

When he appeared on deck he would not speak and not always answer when spoken to. It was obvious that he was ill in some mysterious manner, and beginning to break up.

As the days went by the sounds of the violin became less and less loud, till at last only a feeble scratching would meet Mr. Burns' ear as he stood in the saloon listening outside the door of the captain's state-room.

One afternoon in perfect desperation he burst into that room and made such a scene, tearing his hair and shouting such horrid imprecations that he cowed the contemptuous spirit of the sick man. The water-tanks were low, they had not gained 50 miles in a fortnight. She would never reach Hong-Kong.

It was like fighting desperately towards destruction for the ship and the men. This was evident without argument. Mr. Burns, losing all restraint, put his face close to his captain's and fairly yelled: "You, sir, are going out of the world. But I can't wait till you are dead before I put the helm up. You must do it yourself. You must do it now!"

The man on the couch snarled in contempt: "So I am going out of the world—am I?"

"Yes, sir—you haven't many days left in it," said Mr. Burns calming down. "One can see it by your face."

"My face, eh? . . . Well, put the helm up and be damned to you."

Burns flew on deck, got the ship before the wind, then came down again, composed but resolute.

"I've shaped a course for Pulo Condor,* sir," he said. "When we make it, if you are still with us, you'll tell me into what port you wish me to take the ship and I'll do it."

The old man gave him a look of savage spite, and said these atrocious words in deadly, slow tones:

"If I had my wish, neither the ship nor any of you would ever reach a port. And I hope you won't."

Mr. Burns was profoundly shocked. I believe he was positively frightened at the time. It seems, however, that he managed to produce such an effective laugh that it was the old man's turn to be frightened. He shrank within himself and turned his back on him.

"And his head was not gone then," Mr. Burns assured me excitedly. "He meant every word of it."

Such was practically the late captain's last speech. No connected sentence passed his lips afterwards. That night he used the last of his strength to throw his fiddle over the side. No one had actually seen him in the act, but after his death Mr. Burns couldn't find the thing anywhere. The empty case was very much in evidence, but the fiddle was clearly not in the ship. And where else could it have gone to but overboard?

"Threw his violin overboard!" I exclaimed.

"He did," cried Mr. Burns excitedly. "And it's my belief he would have tried to take the ship down with him if it had been in human power. He never meant her to see home again. He wouldn't write to his owners, he never wrote to his old wife either—he wasn't going to. He had made up his mind to cut adrift from every-thing.* That's what it was. He didn't care for busi-ness, or freights, or for making a passage—or anything. He meant to have gone wandering about the world till he lost her with all hands."

Mr. Burns looked like a man who had escaped great danger. For a little he would have exclaimed: "If it hadn't been for me!" And the transparent innocence of his indignant eyes was underlined quaintly by the arrogant pair of moustaches which he proceeded to twist, and as if extend, horizontally.

I might have smiled if I had not been busy with my own sensations, which were not those of Mr. Burns. I was already the man in command. My sensations could not be like those of any other man on board. In that community I stood, like a king in his country, in a class all by myself. I mean an hereditary king, not a mere elected head of a state. I was brought there to rule by an agency as remote from the people and as inscrut-able almost to them as the Grace of God.

And like a member of a dynasty, feeling a semi-mystical bond with the dead, I was profoundly shocked by my immediate predecessor.

That man had been in all essentials but his age just such another man as myself. Yet the end of his life was a complete act of treason, the betrayal of a tradition which seemed to me as imperative as any guide on earth could be. It appeared that even at sea a man could be-come the victim of evil spirits. I felt on my face the breath of unknown powers that shape our destinies.*

Not to let the silence last too long I asked Mr. Burns if he had written to his captain's wife. He shook his head. He had written to nobody.

In a moment he became sombre. He never thought

of writing. It took him all his time to watch incessantly the loading of the ship by a rascally Chinese stevedore. In this Mr. Burns gave me the first glimpse of the real chief mate's soul which dwelt uneasily in his body.

He mused, then hastened on with gloomy force.

"Yes! The captain died as near noon as possible. I looked through his papers in the afternoon. I read the service over him at sunset and then I stuck the ship's head north and brought her in here. I—brought —her—in."

He struck the table with his fist.

"She would hardly have come in by herself," I observed. "But why didn't you make for Singapore instead?"

His eyes wavered. "The nearest port," he muttered sullenly.

I had framed the question in perfect innocence, but this answer (the difference in distance was insignificant) and his manner offered me a clue to the simple truth. He took the ship to a port where he expected to be confirmed in his temporary command from lack of a qualified master to put over his head. Whereas Singapore, he surmised justly, would be full of qualified men.

But his naïve reasoning forgot to take into account the telegraph cable reposing on the bottom of the very Gulf up which he had turned that ship which he imagined himself to have saved from destruction. Hence the bitter flavour of our interview. I tasted it more and more distinctly—and it was less and less to my taste.

"Look here, Mr. Burns," I began, very firmly. "You may as well understand that I did not run after this command. It was pushed in my way. I've accepted it. I am here to take the ship home first of all, and you may be sure that I shall see to it that every one of you on board here does his duty to that end. This is all I have to say—for the present."

He was on his feet by this time, but instead of taking his dismissal he remained with trembling, indignant lips, and looking at me hard as though, really, after this, there was nothing for me to do in common decency but to vanish from his outraged sight. Like all very simple emotional states this was moving. I felt sorry for him—almost sympathetic, till (seeing that I did not vanish) he spoke in a tone of forced restraint.

"If I hadn't a wife and a child at home you may be sure, sir, I would have asked you to let me go the very minute you came on board."

I answered him with a matter-of-course calmness as though some remote third person were in question.

"And I, Mr. Burns, would not have let you go. You have signed the ship's articles as chief officer, and till they are terminated at the final port of discharge I shall expect you to attend to your duty and give me the benefit of your experience to the best of your ability."

Stony incredulity lingered in his eyes; but it broke down before my friendly attitude. With a slight upward toss of his arms (I got to know that gesture well afterwards) he bolted out of the cabin.

We might have saved ourselves that little passage of harmless sparring. Before many days had elapsed it was Mr. Burns who was pleading with me anxiously not to leave him behind; while I could only return him but doubtful answers. The whole thing took on a somewhat tragic complexion.*

And this horrible problem was only an extraneous episode, a mere complication in the general problem of how to get that ship—which was mine with her appurtenances and her men, with her body and her spirit now slumbering in that pestilential river—how to get her out to sea.

Mr. Burns, while still acting captain, had hastened to sign a charter-party*which in an ideal world without guile would have been an excellent document. Directly I ran my eye over it I foresaw trouble ahead unless the people of the other part were quite exceptionally fair-minded and open to argument.

Mr. Burns, to whom I imparted my fears, chose to take great umbrage at them. He looked at me with that usual incredulous stare, and said bitterly:

"I suppose, sir, you want to make out I've acted like a fool?"

I told him, with my systematic kindliness which always seemed to augment his surprise, that I did not want to make out anything. I would leave that to the future.

And, sure enough, the future brought in a lot of trouble. There were days when I used to remember Captain Giles with nothing short of abhorrence. His confounded acuteness had let me in for this job; while his prophecy that I "would have my hands full" coming true, made it appear as if done on purpose to play an evil joke on my young innocence.

Yes. I had my hands full of complications which were most valuable as "experience." People have a great opinion of the advantages of experience. But in that connection experience means always something disagreeable as opposed to the charm and innocence of illusions.

I must say I was losing mine rapidly. But on these instructive complications I must not enlarge more than to say that they could all be resumed in the one word: Delay.

A mankind which has invented the proverb, "Time

is money," will understand my vexation. The word "Delay" entered the secret chamber of my brain, resounded there like a tolling bell which maddens the ear, affected all my senses, took on a black colouring, a bitter taste, a deadly meaning.

"I am really sorry to see you worried like this. Indeed, I am . . ."

It was the only humane speech I used to hear at that time. And it came from a doctor, appropriately enough.

A doctor is humane by definition. But that man was so in reality. His speech was not professional. I was not ill. But other people were, and that was the reason of his visiting the ship.

He was the doctor of our Legation* and, of course, of the Consulate too. He looked after the ship's health, which generally was poor, and trembling, as it were, on the verge of a break-up. Yes. The men ailed. And thus time was not only money, but life as well.

I had never seen such a steady ship's company. As the doctor remarked to me: "You seem to have a most respectable lot of seamen." Not only were they consistently sober, but they did not even want to go ashore. Care was taken to expose them as little as possible to the sun. They were employed on light work under the awnings. And the humane doctor commended me.

"Your arrangements appear to me to be very judicious, my dear Captain."

It is difficult to express how much that pronouncement comforted me. The doctor's round full face framed in a light-coloured whisker was the perfection of a dignified amenity. He was the only human being in the world who seemed to take the slightest interest in me. He would generally sit in the cabin for half-an-hour or so at every visit.

I said to him one day:

"I suppose the only thing now is to take care of them as you are doing, till I can get the ship to sea?"

He inclined his head, shutting his eyes under the large spectacles, and murmured:

"The sea . . . undoubtedly."

The first member of the crew fairly knocked over was the steward—the first man to whom I had spoken on board. He was taken ashore (with choleraic symptoms)* and died there at the end of a week. Then, while I was still under the startling impression of this first home-thrust of the climate, Mr. Burns gave up and went to bed in a raging fever without saying a word to anybody.

I believe he had partly fretted himself into that illness; the climate did the rest with the swiftness of an invisible monster ambushed in the air, in the water, in the mud of the river bank. Mr. Burns was a pre-destined victim.

I discovered him lying on his back, glaring sullenly and radiating heat on one like a small furnace. He would hardly answer my questions, and only grumbled: Couldn't a man take an afternoon off duty with a bad headache—for once?

That evening, as I sat in the saloon after dinner, I could hear him muttering continuously in his room. Ransome, who was clearing the table, said to me:

"I am afraid, sir, I won't be able to give the mate all the attention he's likely to need. I will have to be forward in the galley a great part of my time."

Ransome was the cook. The mate had pointed him out to me the first day, standing on the deck, his arms crossed on his broad chest, gazing on the river.

Even at a distance his well-proportioned figure, something thoroughly sailor-like in his poise, made him noticeable. On nearer view the intelligent, quiet eyes, a well-bred face, the disciplined independence of his manner made up an attractive personality. When, in addition, Mr. Burns told me that he was the best seaman in the ship, I expressed my surprise that in his earliest prime and of such appearance he should sign on as cook on board a ship.

"It's his heart," Mr. Burns had said. "There's something wrong with it. He mustn't exert himself too much or he may drop dead suddenly."

And he was the only one the climate had not touched —perhaps because, carrying a deadly enemy in his breast, he had schooled himself into a systematic control of feelings and movements. When one was in the secret this was apparent in his manner. After the poor steward died, and as he could not be replaced by a white man in this Oriental port, Ransome had volunteered to do the double work.

"I can do it all right, sir, as long as I go about it quietly," he had assured me.

But obviously he couldn't be expected to take up sick-nursing in addition. Moreover, the doctor peremptorily ordered Mr. Burns ashore.

With a seaman on each side holding him up under the arms, the mate went over the gangway more sullen than ever. We built him up with pillows in the gharry,* and he made an effort to say brokenly:

"Now—you've got—what you wanted—got me out of—the ship."

"You were never more mistaken in your life, Mr. Burns," I said quietly, duly smiling at him; and the trap drove off to a sort of sanatorium, a pavilion of bricks which the doctor had in the grounds of his residence.

I visited Mr. Burns regularly. After the first few

days, when he didn't know anybody, he received me as if I had come either to gloat over a crushed enemy or else to curry favour with a deeply-wronged person. It was either one or the other, just as it happened according to his fantastic sick-room moods. Whichever it was, he managed to convey it to me even during the period when he appeared almost too weak to talk. I treated him to my invariable kindliness.

Then one day, suddenly, a surge of downright panic burst through all this craziness.

If I left him behind in this deadly place he would die. He felt it, he was certain of it. But I wouldn't have the heart to leave him ashore. He had a wife and child in Sydney.

He produced his wasted fore-arms from under the sheet which covered him and clasped his fleshless claws. He would die! He would die here. . . .

He absolutely managed to sit up, but only for a moment, and when he fell back I really thought that he would die there and then. I called to the Bengali dispenser, and hastened away from the room.

Next day he upset me thoroughly by renewing his entreaties. I returned an evasive answer, and left him the picture of ghastly despair. The day after I went in with reluctance, and he attacked me at once in a much stronger voice and with an abundance of argument which was quite startling. He presented his case with a sort of crazy vigour, and asked me finally how would I like to have a man's death on my conscience? He wanted me to promise that I would not sail without him.

I said that I really must consult the doctor first. He cried out at that. The doctor! Never! That would be a death sentence.

The effort had exhausted him. He closed his eyes, but

went on rambling in a low voice. I had hated him from
the start. The late captain had hated him too. Had
wished him dead. Had wished all hands dead. . . .

"What do you want to stand in with that wicked
corpse for, sir? He'll have you too," he ended, blink-
ing his glazed eyes vacantly.

"Mr. Burns," I cried, very much discomposed,
"what on earth are you talking about?"

He seemed to come to himself, though he was too
weak to start.

"I don't know," he said languidly. "But don't ask
that doctor, sir. You and I are sailors. Don't ask
him, sir. Some day perhaps you will have a wife and
child yourself."

And again he pleaded for the promise that I would
not leave him behind. I had the firmness of mind not
to give it to him. Afterwards this sternness seemed
criminal; for my mind was made up. That pros-
trated man, with hardly strength enough to breathe and
ravaged by a passion of fear, was irresistible. And,
besides, he had happened to hit on the right words. He
and I were sailors. That was a claim, for I had no
other family. As to the wife-and-child (some day)
argument it had no force. It sounded merely bizarre.

I could imagine no claim that would be stronger
and more absorbing than the claim of that ship, of these
men snared in the river by silly commercial complications, as if in some poisonous trap.

However, I had nearly fought my way out. Out to
sea. The sea—which was pure, safe, and friendly.
Three days more.

That thought sustained and carried me on my way
back to the ship. In the saloon the doctor's voice
greeted me, and his large form followed his voice, issuing
out of the starboard spare cabin where the ship's

medicine chest was kept securely lashed in the bed-
place.

Finding that I was not on board he had gone in there,
he said, to inspect the supply of drugs, bandages, and so
on. Everything was completed and in order.

I thanked him; I had just been thinking of asking
him to do that very thing, as in a couple of days, as he
knew, we were going to sea, where all our troubles of
every sort would be over at last.

He listened gravely and made no answer. But when
I opened to him my mind as to Mr. Burns he sat down
by my side, and, laying his hand on my knee amicably,
begged me to think what it was I was exposing myself to.

The man was just strong enough to bear being moved
and no more. But he couldn't stand a return of the
fever. I had before me a passage of sixty days perhaps,
beginning with intricate navigation and ending probably with a lot of bad weather. Could I run the risk of
having to go through it single-handed, with no chief
officer and with a second quite a youth? . . .

He might have added that it was my first command
too. He did probably think of that fact, for he checked
himself. It was very present to my mind.

He advised me earnestly to cable to Singapore for a
chief officer, even if I had to delay my sailing for a
week.

"Not a day," I said. The very thought gave me the
shivers. The hands seemed fairly fit, all of them, and
this was the time to get them away. Once at sea I was
not afraid of facing anything. The sea was now the
only remedy for all my troubles.

The doctor's glasses were directed at me like two
lamps searching the genuineness of my resolution. He
opened his lips as if to argue further, but shut them
again without saying anything. I had a vision of poor

Burns so vivid in his exhaustion, helplessness, and anguish, that it moved me more than the reality I had come away from only an hour before. It was purged from the drawbacks of his personality, and I could not resist it.

"Look here," I said. "Unless you tell me officially that the man must not be moved I'll make arrangements to have him brought on board to-morrow, and shall take the ship out of the river next morning, even if I have to anchor outside the bar for a couple of days to get her ready for sea."

"Oh! I'll make all the arrangements myself," said the doctor at once. "I spoke as I did only as a friend—as a well-wisher, and that sort of thing."

He rose in his dignified simplicity and gave me a warm handshake, rather solemnly, I thought. But he was as good as his word. When Mr. Burns appeared at the gangway carried on a stretcher, the doctor himself walked by its side. The programme had been altered in so far that this transportation had been left to the last moment, on the very morning of our departure.

It was barely an hour after sunrise. The doctor waved his big arm to me from the shore and walked back at once to his trap, which had followed him empty to the river-side. Mr. Burns, carried across the quarter-deck, had the appearance of being absolutely lifeless. Ransome went down to settle him in his cabin. I had to remain on deck to look after the ship, for the tug had got hold of our tow-rope already.

The splash of our shore-fasts falling in the water produced a complete change of feeling in me. It was like the imperfect relief of awakening from a nightmare. But when the ship's head swung down the river away from that town, Oriental and squalid, I missed the expected elation of that striven-for moment. What there was, undoubtedly, was a relaxation of tension which translated itself into a sense of weariness after an inglorious fight.*

About mid-day we anchored a mile outside the bar. The afternoon was busy for all hands. Watching the work from the poop, where I remained all the time, I detected in it some of the languor of the six weeks spent in the steaming heat of the river. The first breeze would blow that away. Now the calm was complete. I judged that the second officer—a callow youth with an unpromising face—was not, to put it mildly, of that invaluable stuff from which a commander's right hand is made. But I was glad to catch along the main deck a few smiles on those seamen's faces at which I had hardly had time to have a good look as yet. Having thrown off the mortal coil*of shore affairs, I felt myself familiar with them and yet a little strange, like a long-lost wanderer among his kin.

Ransome flitted continually to and fro between the galley and the cabin. It was a pleasure to look at him. The man positively had grace. He alone of all the crew had not had a day's illness in port. But with the knowledge of that uneasy heart within his breast I could detect the restraint he put on the natural sailor-like agility of his movements. It was as though he had something very fragile or very explosive to carry about his person and was all the time aware of it.

I had occasion to address him once or twice. He answered me in his pleasant quiet voice and with a faint, slightly wistful smile. Mr. Burns appeared to be resting. He seemed fairly comfortable.

After sunset I came out on deck again to meet only a still void. The thin, featureless crust of the coast could not be distinguished. The darkness had risen around the ship like a mysterious emanation from the dumb and

lonely waters. I leaned on the rail and turned my ear
to the shadows of the night. Not a sound. My command might have been a planet flying vertiginously on
its appointed path in a space of infinite silence. I
clung to the rail as if my sense of balance were leaving
me for good. How absurd. I hailed nervously.

"On deck there!"

The immediate answer, "Yes, sir," broke the spell.
The anchor-watch*man ran up the poop ladder smartly.
I told him to report at once the slightest sign of a breeze
coming.

Going below I looked in on Mr. Burns. In fact, I
could not avoid seeing him, for his door stood open.
The man was so wasted that, in that white cabin, under
a white sheet, and with his diminished head sunk in the
white pillow, his red moustaches captured one's eyes
exclusively, like something artificial—a pair of moustaches from a shop exhibited there in the harsh light of
the bulkhead-lamp without a shade.

While I stared with a sort of wonder he asserted himself by opening his eyes and even moving them in my
direction. A minute stir.

"Dead calm, Mr. Burns," I said resignedly.

In an unexpectedly distinct voice Mr. Burns began a
rambling speech. Its tone was very strange, not as if
affected by his illness, but as if of a different nature. It
sounded unearthly. As to the matter, I seemed to
make out that it was the fault of the "old man"—the
late captain—ambushed down there under the sea with
some evil intention. It was a weird story.

I listened to the end; then stepping into the cabin I
laid my hand on the mate's forehead. It was cool. He
was light-headed only from extreme weakness. Suddenly he seemed to become aware of me, and in his own
voice—of course, very feeble—he asked regretfully:

"Is there no chance at all to get under way, sir?"

"What's the good of letting go our hold of the ground only to drift, Mr. Burns?" I answered.*

He sighed, and I left him to his immobility. His hold on life was as slender as his hold on sanity. I was oppressed by my lonely responsibilities.* I went into my cabin to seek relief in a few hours' sleep, but almost before I closed my eyes the man on deck came down reporting a light breeze. Enough to get under way with, he said.

And it was no more than just enough. I ordered the windlass*manned, the sails loosed, and the topsails set. But by the time I had cast the ship I could hardly feel any breath of wind. Nevertheless, I trimmed the yards*and put everything on her. I was not going to give up the attempt.

IV

WITH her anchor at the bow and clothed in canvas to her very trucks,* my command seemed to stand as motionless as a model ship set on the gleams and shadows of polished marble. It was impossible to distinguish land from water in the enigmatical tranquillity of the immense forces of the world. A sudden impatience possessed me.

"Won't she answer the helm at all?" I said irritably to the man whose strong brown hands grasping the spokes of the wheel stood out lighted on the darkness; like a symbol of mankind's claim to the direction of its own fate.

He answered me:

"Yes, sir. She's coming-to slowly."

"Let her head come up to south."

"Aye, aye, sir."

I paced the poop. There was not a sound but that of my footsteps, till the man spoke again.

"She is at south now, sir."

I felt a slight tightness of the chest before I gave out the first course of my first command to the silent night, heavy with dew and sparkling with stars. There was a finality in the act committing me to the endless vigilance of my lonely task.

"Steady her head at that," I said at last. "The course is south."

"South, sir," echoed the man.

I sent below the second mate and his watch and remained in charge, walking the deck through the chill, somnolent hours that precede the dawn.

Slight puffs came and went, and whenever they were strong enough to wake up the black water the murmur alongside ran through my very heart in a delicate crescendo of delight and died away swiftly. I was bitterly tired. The very stars seemed weary of waiting for daybreak. It came at last with a mother-of-pearl sheen at the zenith,* such as I had never seen before in the tropics, unglowing, almost grey, with a strange reminder of high latitudes.

The voice of the look-out man hailed from forward:

"Land on the port bow, sir."

"All right."

Leaning on the rail I never even raised my eyes. The motion of the ship was imperceptible. Presently Ransome brought me the cup of morning coffee. After I drunk it I looked ahead, and in the still streak of very bright pale orange light I saw the land profiled flatly as if cut out of black paper and seeming to float on the water as light as cork. But the rising sun turned it into mere dark vapour, a doubtful, massive shadow trembling in the hot glare.

The watch finished washing decks. I went below and stopped at Mr. Burns' door (he could not bear to have it shut), but hesitated to speak to him till he moved his eyes. I gave him the news.

"Sighted Cape Liant* at daylight. About fifteen miles."

He moved his lips then, but I heard no sound till I put my ear down, and caught the peevish comment: "This is crawling. . . . No luck."

"Better luck than standing still, anyhow," I pointed out resignedly, and left him to whatever thoughts or fancies haunted his hopeless prostration.

Later that morning, when relieved by my second officer, I threw myself on my couch and for some three hours or so I really found oblivion. It was so perfect that on waking up I wondered where I was. Then came the immense relief of the thought: on board my ship! At sea! At sea!

Through the port-holes I beheld an unruffled, sun-smitten horizon. The horizon of a windless day. But its spaciousness alone was enough to give me a sense of a fortunate escape, a momentary exultation of freedom.

I stepped out into the saloon with my heart lighter than it had been for days. Ransome was at the side-board preparing to lay the table for the first sea dinner of the passage. He turned his head, and something in his eyes checked my modest elation.

Instinctively I asked: "What is it now?" not expecting in the least the answer I got. It was given with that sort of contained serenity which was characteristic of the man.

"I am afraid we haven't left all sickness behind us, sir."

"We haven't! What's the matter?"

He told me then that two of our men had been taken bad with fever in the night. One of them was burning and the other was shivering, but he thought that it was pretty much the same thing. I thought so too. I felt shocked by the news. "One burning, the other shivering, you say? No. We haven't left the sickness behind. Do they look very ill?"

"Middling bad, sir." Ransome's eyes gazed steadily into mine. We exchanged smiles. Ransome's a little wistful, as usual, mine no doubt grim enough, to correspond with my secret exasperation.

I asked:

"Was there any wind at all this morning?"

"Can hardly say that, sir. We've moved all the time though. The land ahead seems a little nearer."

That was it. A little nearer. Whereas if we had only had a little more wind, only a very little more, we might, we should, have been abreast of Liant by this time and increasing our distance from that contaminated shore. And it was not only the distance. It seemed to me that a stronger breeze would have blown away the infection which clung to the ship. It obviously did cling to the ship. Two men. One burning, one shivering. I felt a distinct reluctance to go and look at them. What was the good? Poison is poison. Tropical fever is tropical fever. But that it should have stretched its claw after us over the sea seemed to me an extraordinary and unfair licence. I could hardly believe that it could be anything worse than the last desperate pluck of the evil from which we were escaping into the clean breath of the sea. If only that breath had been a little stronger. However, there was the quinine against the fever. I went into the spare cabin where the medicine chest was kept to prepare two doses. I opened it full of faith as a man opens a miraculous shrine. The upper part was inhabited by a collection of bottles, all square-shouldered and as like each other as peas. Under that orderly array there were two drawers, stuffed as full of things as one could imagine—paper packages, bandages, cardboard boxes officially labelled. The lower of the two, in one of its compartments, contained our provision of quinine.

There were five bottles, all round and all of a size. One was about a third full. The other four remained still wrapped up in paper and sealed. But I did not expect to see an envelope lying on top of them. A square envelope, belonging, in fact, to the ship's stationery.

It lay so that I could see it was not closed down, and on picking it up and turning it over I perceived that it was addressed to myself. It contained a half-sheet of notepaper, which I unfolded with a queer sense of dealing with the uncanny, but without any excitement as people meet and do extraordinary things in a dream.

"My dear Captain," it began, but I ran to the signature. The writer was the doctor. The date was that of the day on which, returning from my visit to Mr. Burns in the hospital, I had found the excellent doctor waiting for me in the cabin; and when he told me that he had been putting in time inspecting the medicine chest for me. How bizarre! While expecting me to come in at any moment he had been amusing himself by writing me a letter, and then as I came in had hastened to stuff it into the medicine chest drawer. A rather incredible proceeding. I turned to the text in wonder.

In a large, hurried, but legible hand the good, sympathetic man for some reason, either of kindness or more likely impelled by the irresistible desire to express his opinion, with which he didn't want to damp my hopes before, was warning me not to put my trust in the beneficial effects of a change from land to sea. "I didn't want to add to your worries by discouraging your hopes," he wrote. "I am afraid that, medically speaking, the end of your troubles is not yet." In short, he expected me to have to fight a probable return of tropical illness. Fortunately I had a good provision of quinine. I should put my trust in that, and administer it steadily, when the ship's health would certainly improve.

I crumpled up the letter and rammed it into my pocket. Ransome carried off two big doses to the men forward. As to myself, I did not go on deck as yet. I went instead to the door of Mr. Burns' room, and gave him that news too.

It was impossible to say the effect it had on him. At first I thought that he was speechless. His head lay sunk in the pillow. He moved his lips enough, however, to assure me that he was getting much stronger; a statement shockingly untrue on the face of it.

That afternoon I took my watch as a matter of course. A great over-heated stillness enveloped the ship and seemed to hold her motionless in a flaming ambience composed in two shades of blue. Faint, hot puffs eddied nervelessly from her sails. And yet she moved. She must have. For, as the sun was setting, we had drawn abreast of Cape Liant and dropped it behind us: an ominous retreating shadow in the last gleams of twilight.

In the evening, under the crude glare of his lamp, Mr. Burns seemed to have come more to the surface of his bedding. It was as if a depressing hand had been lifted off him. He answered my few words by a comparatively long, connected speech. He asserted himself strongly. If he escaped being smothered by this stagnant heat, he said, he was confident that in a very few days he would be able to come up on deck and help me.

While he was speaking I trembled lest this effort of energy should leave him lifeless before my eyes. But I cannot deny that there was something comforting in his willingness. I made a suitable reply, but pointed out to him that the only thing that could really help us was wind—a fair wind.

He rolled his head impatiently on the pillow. And it was not comforting in the least to hear him begin to mutter crazily about the late captain, that old man buried in latitude 8° 20′, right in our way—ambushed at the entrance of the Gulf.

"Are you still thinking of your late captain, Mr. Burns?" I said. "I imagine the dead feel no animosity against the living. They care nothing for them."

"You don't know that one," he breathed out feebly.

"No. I didn't know him, and he didn't know me. And so he can't have any grievance against me, anyway."

"Yes. But there's all the rest of us on board," he insisted.

I felt the inexpugnable strength of common sense being insidiously menaced by this gruesome, by this insane delusion. And I said:

"You mustn't talk so much. You will tire yourself."

"And there is the ship herself," he persisted in a whisper.

"Now, not a word more," I said, stepping in and laying my hand on his cool forehead. It proved to me that this atrocious absurdity was rooted in the man himself and not in the disease, which, apparently, had emptied him of every power, mental and physical, except that one fixed idea.

I avoided giving Mr. Burns any opening for conversation for the next few days. I merely used to throw him a hasty, cheery word when passing his door. I believe that if he had had the strength he would have called out after me more than once. But he hadn't the strength. Ransome, however, observed to me one afternoon that the mate "seemed to be picking up wonderfully."

"Did he talk any nonsense to you of late?" I asked casually.

"No, sir." Ransome was startled by the direct question; but, after a pause, he added equably: "He told me this morning, sir, that he was sorry he had to bury our late captain right in the ship's way,* as one may say, out of the Gulf."

"Isn't this nonsense enough for you?" I asked, looking confidently at the intelligent, quiet face on which the secret uneasiness in the man's breast had thrown a transparent veil of care.

Ransome didn't know. He had not given a thought to the matter. And with a faint smile he flitted away from me on his never-ending duties, with his usual guarded activity.

Two more days passed. We had advanced a little way—a very little way—into the larger space of the Gulf of Siam. Seizing eagerly upon the elation of the first command thrown into my lap, by the agency of Captain Giles, I had yet an uneasy feeling that such luck as this has got perhaps to be paid for in some way. I had held, professionally, a review of my chances. I was competent enough for that. At least, I thought so.* I had a general sense of my preparedness which only a man pursuing a calling he loves can know. That feeling seemed to me the most natural thing in the world. As natural as breathing. I imagined I could not have lived without it.

I don't know what I expected. Perhaps nothing else than that special intensity of existence which is the quintessence of youthful aspirations. Whatever I expected I did not expect to be beset by hurricanes. I knew better than that. In the Gulf of Siam there are no hurricanes. But neither did I expect to find myself bound hand and foot to the hopeless extent which was revealed to me as the days went on.

Not that the evil spell held us always motionless. Mysterious currents drifted us here and there, with a stealthy power made manifest by the changing vistas of the islands fringing the east shore of the Gulf. And there were winds too, fitful and deceitful. They raised hopes only to dash them into the bitterest disappointment, promises of advance ending in lost ground, expiring in sighs, dying into dumb stillness in which the currents had it all their own way—their own inimical way.

The Island of Koh-ring,* a great, black, upheaved ridge amongst a lot of tiny islets, lying upon the glassy water like a triton amongst minnows, seemed to be the centre of the fatal circle. It seemed impossible to get away from it. Day after day it remained in sight. More than once, in a favourable breeze, I would take its bearing in the fast ebbing twilight, thinking that it was for the last time. Vain hope. A night of fitful airs would undo the gains of temporary favour, and the rising sun would throw out the black relief of Koh-ring, looking more barren, inhospitable, and grim than ever.

"It's like being bewitched, upon my word," I said once to Mr. Burns, from my usual position in the doorway.

He was sitting up in his bed-place. He was progressing towards the world of living men; if he could hardly have been said to have rejoined it yet. He nodded to me his frail and bony head in a wisely mysterious assent.

"Oh, yes, I know what you mean," I said. "But you cannot expect me to believe that a dead man has the power to put out of joint the meteorology of this part of the world. Though indeed it seems to have gone utterly wrong. The land and sea breezes have got broken up into small pieces. We cannot depend upon them for five minutes together."

"It won't be very long now before I can come up on deck," muttered Mr. Burns, "and then we shall see."

Whether he meant this for a promise to grapple with supernatural evil I couldn't tell. At any rate, it wasn't the kind of assistance I needed. On the other hand, I had been living on deck practically night and day so as to take advantage of every chance to get my ship a little more to the southward. The mate, I could see, was extremely weak yet, and not quite rid of his delusion, which to me appeared but a symptom of his disease. At all events, the hopefulness of an invalid was not to be discouraged. I said:

"You will be most welcome there, I am sure, Mr. Burns. If you go on improving at this rate you'll be presently one of the healthiest men in the ship."

This pleased him, but his extreme emaciation converted his self-satisfied smile into a ghastly exhibition of long teeth under the red moustache.

"Aren't the fellows improving, sir?" he asked soberly, with an extremely sensible expression of anxiety on his face.

I answered him only with a vague gesture and went away from the door. The fact was that disease played with us capriciously very much as the winds did. It would go from one man to another with a lighter or heavier touch, which always left its mark behind, staggering some, knocking others over for a time, leaving this one, returning to another, so that all of them had now an invalidish aspect and a hunted, apprehensive look in their eyes; while Ransome and I, the only two completely untouched, went amongst them assiduously distributing quinine. It was a double fight. The adverse weather held us in front and the disease pressed on our rear. I must say that the men were very good. The constant toil of trimming the yards they faced willingly. But all spring was out of their limbs, and as I looked at them from the poop I could not keep from my mind the dreadful impression that they were moving in poisoned air.

Down below, in his cabin, Mr. Burns had advanced so far as not only to be able to sit up, but even to draw up his legs. Clasping them with bony arms, like an animated skeleton, he emitted deep, impatient sighs.

"The great thing to do, sir," he would tell me on every occasion, when I gave him the chance, "the great thing is to get the ship past 8° 20′ of latitude. Once she's past that we're all right."

At first I used only to smile at him, though, God knows, I had not much heart left for smiles. But at last I lost my patience.

"Oh, yes. The latitude 8° 20′. That's where you buried your late captain, isn't it?" Then with severity: "Don't you think, Mr. Burns, it's about time you dropped all that nonsense?"

He rolled at me his deep-sunken eyes in a glance of invincible obstinacy. But for the rest, he only muttered, just loud enough for me to hear, something about "Not surprised . . . find . . . play us some beastly trick yet . . ."

Such passages as this were not exactly wholesome for my resolution. The stress of adversity was beginning to tell on me. At the same time I felt a contempt for that obscure weakness of my soul. I said to myself disdainfully that it should take much more than that to affect in the smallest degree my fortitude.

I didn't know then how soon and from what unexpected direction it would be attacked.

It was the very next day. The sun had risen clear of the southern shoulder of Koh-ring, which still hung, like an evil attendant, on our port quarter. It was intensely hateful to my sight. During the night we had been heading all round the compass, trimming the yards again and again, to what I fear must have been for the most part imaginary puffs of air. Then just about sunrise we got for an hour an inexplicable, steady breeze, right in our teeth. There was no sense in it. It fitted neither with the season of the year, nor with the secular experience of seamen as recorded in books, nor with the aspect of the sky. Only purposeful malevolence could account for it. It sent us travelling at a great pace away from our proper course; and if we had been out on pleasure sailing bent it would have been a delightful breeze, with the awakened sparkle of the sea, with the sense of motion and a feeling of unwonted freshness. Then all at once, as if disdaining to carry farther the sorry jest, it dropped and died out completely in less than five minutes. The ship's head swung where it listed; the stilled sea took on the polish of a steel plate in the calm.

I went below, not because I meant to take some rest, but simply because I couldn't bear to look at it just then. The indefatigable Ransome was busy in the saloon. It had become a regular practice with him to give me an informal health report in the morning. He turned away from the sideboard with his usual pleasant, quiet gaze. No shadow rested on his intelligent forehead.

"There are a good many of them middling bad this morning, sir," he said in a calm tone.

"What? All knocked out?"

"Only two actually in their bunks, sir, but . . ."

"It's the last night that has done for them. We have had to pull and haul all the blessed time."

"I heard, sir. I had a mind to come out and help only, you know. . . ."

"Certainly not. You mustn't. . . . The fellows

lie at night about the decks, too. It isn't good for
them."

Ransome assented. But men couldn't be looked
after like children. Moreover, one could hardly blame
them for trying for such coolness and such air as there
was to be found on deck. He himself, of course, knew
better.

He was, indeed, a reasonable man. Yet it would
have been hard to say that the others were not. The
last few days had been for us like the ordeal of the fiery
furnace. One really couldn't quarrel with their common, imprudent humanity making the best of the
moments of relief, when the night brought in the illusion
of coolness and the starlight twinkled through the
heavy, dew-laden air. Moreover, most of them were so
weakened that hardly anything could be done without
everybody that could totter mustering on the braces.*
No, it was no use remonstrating with them. But I
fully believed that quinine was of very great use indeed.

I believed in it. I pinned my faith to it. It would
save the men, the ship, break the spell by its medicinal
virtue, make time of no account, the weather but a
passing worry, and, like a magic powder working
against mysterious malefices,* secure the first passage of
my first command against the evil powers of calms and
pestilence. I looked upon it as more precious than
gold, and unlike gold, of which there ever hardly seems
to be enough anywhere, the ship had a sufficient store
of it. I went in to get it with the purpose of weighing
out doses. I stretched my hand with the feeling of a
man reaching for an unfailing panacea, took up a fresh
bottle and unrolled the wrapper, noticing as I did so
that the ends, both top and bottom, had come un-
sealed. . . .

But why record all the swift steps of the appalling

discovery. You have guessed the truth already. There was the wrapper, the bottle, and the white powder inside, some sort of powder! But it wasn't quinine. One look at it was quite enough. I remember that at the very moment of picking up the bottle, before I even dealt with the wrapper, the weight of the object I had in my hand gave me an instant of premonition. Quinine is as light as feathers; and my nerves must have been exasperated into an extraordinary sensibility. I let the bottle smash itself on the floor. The stuff, whatever it was, felt gritty under the sole of my shoe. I snatched up the next bottle and then the next. The weight alone told the tale. One after another they fell, breaking at my feet, not because I threw them down in my dismay, but slipping through my fingers as if this disclosure were too much for my strength.

It is a fact that the very greatness of a mental shock helps one to bear up against it, by producing a sort of temporary insensibility. I came out of the state-room stunned, as if something heavy had dropped on my head. From the other side of the saloon, across the table, Ransome, with a duster in his hand, stared open-mouthed. I don't think that I looked wild. It is quite possible that I appeared to be in a hurry because I was instinctively hastening up on deck. An example this of training become instinct. The difficulties, the dangers, the problems of a ship at sea must be met on deck.

To this fact, as it were of nature, I responded instinctively; which may be taken as a proof that for a moment I must have been robbed of my reason.

I was certainly off my balance, a prey to impulse, for at the bottom of the stairs I turned and flung myself at the doorway of Mr. Burns' cabin. The wildness of his aspect checked my mental disorder. He was sitting up in his bunk, his body looking immensely long, his head drooping a little sideways, with affected complacency. He flourished, in his trembling hand, on the end of a fore-arm no thicker than a stout walking-stick, a shining pair of scissors which he tried before my very eyes to jab at his throat.

I was to a certain extent horrified; but it was rather a secondary sort of effect, not really strong enough to make me yell at him in some such manner as: "Stop!" . . . "Heavens!" . . . "What are you doing?"

In reality he was simply overtaxing his returning strength in a shaky attempt to clip off the thick growth of his red beard. A large towel was spread over his lap, and a shower of stiff hairs, like bits of copper wire, was descending on it at every snip of the scissors.

He turned to me his face grotesque beyond the fantasies of mad dreams, one cheek all bushy as if with a swollen flame, the other denuded and sunken, with the untouched long moustache on that side asserting itself, lonely and fierce. And while he stared thunderstruck, with the gaping scissors on his fingers, I shouted my discovery at him fiendishly, in six words, without comment.

V

I HEARD the clatter of the scissors escaping from his hand, noted the perilous heave of his whole person over the edge of the bunk after them, and then, returning to my first purpose, pursued my course on to the deck. The sparkle of the sea filled my eyes. It was gorgeous and barren, monotonous and without hope under the empty curve of the sky. The sails hung motionless and slack, the very folds of their sagging surfaces moved no more than carved granite. The impetuosity of my advent made the man at the helm start slightly. A block aloft squeaked incomprehensibly, for what on earth could have made it do so? It was a whistling note like a bird's. For a long, long time I faced an empty world, steeped in an infinity of silence, through which the sunshine poured and flowed for some mysterious purpose. Then I heard Ransome's voice at my elbow.

"I have put Mr. Burns back to bed, sir."

"You have."

"Well, sir, he got out, all of a sudden, but when he let go of the edge of his bunk he fell down. He isn't light-headed, though, it seems to me."

"No," I said dully, without looking at Ransome. He waited for a moment, then, cautiously as if not to give offence: "I don't think we need lose much of that stuff, sir," he said, "I can sweep it up, every bit of it almost, and then we could sift the glass out. I will go about it at once. It will not make the breakfast late, not ten minutes."

"Oh, yes," I said bitterly. "Let the breakfast wait,

sweep up every bit of it, and then throw the damned lot overboard!"

The profound silence returned, and when I looked over my shoulder Ransome—the intelligent, serene Ransome—had vanished from my side. The intense loneliness of the sea acted like poison on my brain. When I turned my eyes to the ship, I had a morbid vision of her as a floating grave. Who hasn't heard of ships found drifting, haphazard, with their crews all dead?* I looked at the seaman at the helm, I had an impulse to speak to him, and, indeed, his face took on an expectant cast as if he had guessed my intention. But in the end I went below, thinking I would be alone with the greatness of my trouble for a little while. But through his open door Mr. Burns saw me come down, and addressed me grumpily: "Well, sir?"

I went in. "It isn't well at all," I said.

Mr. Burns, re-established in his bed-place, was concealing his hirsute cheek in the palm of his hand.

"That confounded fellow has taken away the scissors from me," were the next words he said.

The tension I was suffering from was so great that it was perhaps just as well that Mr. Burns had started on this grievance. He seemed very sore about it and grumbled, "Does he think I am mad, or what?"

"I don't think so, Mr. Burns," I said. I looked upon him at that moment as a model of self-possession. I even conceived on that account a sort of admiration for that man, who had (apart from the intense materiality of what was left of his beard) come as near to being a disembodied spirit as any man can do and live. I noticed the preternatural sharpness of the ridge of his nose, the deep cavities of his temples, and I envied him. He was so reduced that he would probably die very soon. Enviable man! So near extinction—while I had to bear within me a tumult of suffering vitality, doubt, confusion, self-reproach, and an indefinite reluctance to meet the horrid logic of the situation. I could not help muttering: "I feel as if I were going mad myself."

Mr. Burns glared spectrally, but otherwise wonderfully composed.

"I always thought he would play us some deadly trick," he said, with a peculiar emphasis on the *he*.

It gave me a mental shock, but I had neither the mind, nor the heart, nor the spirit to argue with him. My form of sickness was indifference. The creeping paralysis of a hopeless outlook. So I only gazed at him. Mr. Burns broke into further speech.

"Eh? What? No! You won't believe it? Well, how do you account for this? How do you think it could have happened?"

"Happened?" I repeated dully. "Why, yes, how in the name of the infernal powers did this thing happen?"

Indeed, on thinking it out, it seemed incomprehensible that it should just be like this: the bottles emptied, refilled, rewrapped, and replaced. A sort of plot, a sinister attempt to deceive, a thing resembling sly vengeance—but for what?—or else a fiendish joke. But Mr. Burns was in possession of a theory. It was simple, and he uttered it solemnly in a hollow voice.

"I suppose they have given him about fifteen pounds in Haiphong for that little lot."

"Mr. Burns!" I cried.

He nodded grotesquely over his raised legs, like two broomsticks in the pyjamas, with enormous bare feet at the end.

"Why not? The stuff is pretty expensive in this

part of the world, and they were very short of it in Tonkin. And what did he care? You have not known him. I have, and I have defied him. He feared neither God, nor devil, nor man, nor wind, nor sea, nor his own conscience. And I believe he hated everybody and everything. But I think he was afraid to die. I believe I am the only man who ever stood up to him. I faced him in that cabin where you live now, when he was sick, and I cowed him then. He thought I was going to twist his neck for him. If he had had his way we would have been beating up against the North-East monsoon, as long as he lived and afterwards too, for ages and ages. Acting the Flying Dutchman in the China Sea! Ha! Ha!"

"But why should he replace the bottles like this?" . . . I began.

"Why shouldn't he? Why should he want to throw the bottles away? They fit the drawer. They belong to the medicine chest."

"And they were wrapped up," I cried.

"Well, the wrappers were there. Did it from habit, I suppose, and as to refilling, there is always a lot of stuff they send in paper parcels that burst after a time. And then, who can tell? I suppose you didn't taste it, sir? But, of course, you are sure . . ."

"No," I said. "I didn't taste it. It is all overboard now."

Behind me, a soft, cultivated voice said: "I have tasted it. It seemed a mixture of all sorts, sweetish, saltish, very horrible."

Ransome, stepping out of the pantry, had been listening for some time, as it was very excusable in him to do.

"A dirty trick," said Mr. Burns. "I always said he would."

The magnitude of my indignation was unbounded. And the kind, sympathetic doctor too. The only sympathetic man I ever knew . . . instead of writing that warning letter, the very refinement of sympathy, why didn't the man make a proper inspection? But, as a matter of fact, it was hardly fair to blame the doctor. The fittings were in order and the medicine chest is an officially arranged affair. There was nothing really to arouse the slightest suspicion. The person I could never forgive was myself. Nothing should ever be taken for granted. The seed of everlasting remorse was sown in my breast.

"I feel it's all my fault," I exclaimed, "mine, and nobody else's. That's how I feel. I shall never forgive myself."

"That's very foolish, sir," said Mr. Burns fiercely.

And after this effort he fell back exhausted on his bed. He closed his eyes, he panted; this affair, this abominable surprise had shaken him up too. As I turned away I perceived Ransome looking at me blankly. He appreciated what it meant, but he managed to produce his pleasant, wistful smile. Then he stepped back into his pantry, and I rushed up on deck again to see whether there was any wind, any breath under the sky, any stir of the air, any sign of hope. The deadly stillness met me again. Nothing was changed except that there was a different man at the wheel. He looked ill. His whole figure drooped, and he seemed rather to cling to the spokes than hold them with a controlling grip. I said to him:

"You are not fit to be here."

"I can manage, sir," he said feebly.

As a matter of fact, there was nothing for him to do. The ship had no steerage way. She lay with her head to the westward, the everlasting Koh-ring visible over

the stern, with a few small islets, black spots in the great
blaze, swimming before my troubled eyes. And but
for those bits of land there was no speck on the sky, no
speck on the water, no shape of vapour, no wisp of
smoke, no sail, no boat, no stir of humanity, no sign
of life, nothing!

The first question was, what to do? What could
one do? The first thing to do obviously was to tell
the men. I did it that very day. I wasn't going to
let the knowledge simply get about. I would face
them. They were assembled on the quarter-deck* for
the purpose. Just before I stepped out to speak to
them I discovered that life could hold terrible moments.
No confessed criminal had ever been so oppressed by
his sense of guilt. This is why, perhaps, my face was
set hard and my voice curt and unemotional while I
made my declaration that I could do nothing more for
the sick, in the way of drugs. As to such care as could
be given them they knew they had had it.

I would have held them justified in tearing me limb
from limb. The silence which followed upon my words
was almost harder to bear than the angriest uproar. I
was crushed by the infinite depth of its reproach. But,
as a matter of fact, I was mistaken. In a voice which
I had great difficulty in keeping firm, I went on: "I
suppose, men, you have understood what I said, and
you know what it means."

A voice or two were heard: "Yes, sir . . . . We
understand."

They had kept silent simply because they thought
that they were not called to say anything; and when I
told them that I intended to run into Singapore and
that the best chance for the ship and the men was in
the efforts all of us, sick and well, must make to get
her along out of this, I received the encouragement of a

low assenting murmur and of a louder voice exclaiming:
"Surely there is a way out of this blamed hole."

*   *   *

Here is an extract from the notes I wrote at the time:

We have lost Koh-ring at last. For many days now I don't
think I have been two hours below altogether. I remain on deck, of
course, night and day, and the nights and the days wheel over us in
succession, whether long or short, who can say? All sense of time
is lost in the monotony of expectation, of hope, and of desire—which
is only one: Get the ship to the southward! Get the ship to the
southward! The effect is curiously mechanical; the sun climbs
and descends, the night swings over our heads as if somebody below
the horizon were turning a crank. It is the pettiest, the most aim-
less! . . . and all through that miserable performance I go on,
tramping, tramping the deck. How many miles have I walked
on the poop of that ship! A stubborn pilgrimage of sheer restless-
ness, diversified by short excursions below to look upon Mr. Burns.
I don't know whether it is an illusion, but he seems to become more
substantial from day to day. He doesn't say much, for, indeed, the
situation doesn't lend itself to idle remarks. I notice this even
with the men as I watch them moving or sitting about the decks.
They don't talk to each other. It strikes me that if there exist an
invisible ear catching the whispers of the earth, it will find this ship
the most silent spot on it. . . .

No, Mr. Burns has not much to say to me. He sits in his bunk
with his beard gone, his moustaches flaming, and with an air of
silent determination on his chalky physiognomy. Ransome tells
me he devours all the food that is given him to the last scrap, but
that, apparently, he sleeps very little. Even at night, when I go
below to fill my pipe, I notice that, though dozing flat on his back,
he still looks very determined. From the side glance he gives me
when awake it seems as though he were annoyed at being interrupted
in some arduous mental operation; and as I emerge on deck the
ordered arrangement of the stars meets my eye, unclouded, infinitely
wearisome. There they are: stars, sun, sea, light, darkness, space,
great waters; the formidable Work of the Seven Days, into which
mankind seems to have blundered unbidden. Or else decoyed.

Even as I have been decoyed into this awful, this death-haunted
command. . . .

*   *   *

The only spot of light in the ship at night was that
of the compass-lamps, lighting up the faces of the suc-
ceeding helmsmen; for the rest we were lost in the darkness, I walking the poop and the men lying about the
decks. They were all so reduced by sickness that no
watches could be kept. Those who were able to walk
remained all the time on duty, lying about in the
shadows of the main deck, till my voice raised for an
order would bring them to their enfeebled feet, a tottering little group, moving patiently about the ship, with
hardly a murmur, a whisper amongst them all. And
every time I had to raise my voice it was with a pang
of remorse and pity.

Then about four o'clock in the morning a light would
gleam forward in the galley. The unfailing Ransome
with the uneasy heart, immune, serene, and active,
was getting ready the early coffee for the men. Presently he would bring me a cup up on the poop, and
it was then that I allowed myself to drop into my deck
chair for a couple of hours of real sleep. No doubt I
must have been snatching short dozes when leaning
against the rail for a moment in sheer exhaustion; but,
honestly, I was not aware of them, except in the painful form of convulsive starts that seemed to come on me
even while I walked. From about five, however, until
after seven I would sleep openly under the fading stars.

I would say to the helmsman: "Call me at need,"
and drop into that chair and close my eyes, feeling that
there was no more sleep for me on earth. And then
I would know nothing till, some time between seven

and eight, I would feel a touch on my shoulder and look up at Ransome's face, with its faint, wistful smile and friendly, grey eyes, as though he were tenderly amused at my slumbers. Occasionally the second mate would come up and relieve me at early coffee time. But it didn't really matter. Generally it was a dead calm, or else faint airs so changing and fugitive that it really wasn't worth while to touch a brace for them. If the air steadied at all the seaman at the helm could be trusted for a warning shout: "Ship's all aback,* sir!" which like a trumpet-call would make me spring a foot above the deck. Those were the words which it seemed to me would have made me spring up from eternal sleep. But this was not often. I have never met since such breathless sunrises. And if the second mate happened to be there (he had generally one day in three free of fever) I would find him sitting on the skylight half-senseless, as it were, and with an idiotic gaze fastened on some object near by—a rope, a cleat,* a belaying pin,* a ringbolt.*

That young man was rather troublesome. He remained cubbish in his sufferings. He seemed to have become completely imbecile; and when the return of fever drove him to his cabin below the next thing would be that we would miss him from there. The first time it happened Ransome and I were very much alarmed. We started a quiet search and ultimately Ransome discovered him curled up in the sail-locker, which opened into the lobby by a sliding-door. When remonstrated with, he muttered sulkily, "It's cool in there." That wasn't true. It was only dark there.

The fundamental defects of his face were not improved by its uniform livid hue. It was not so with many of the men. The wastage of ill-health seemed to idealize the general character of the features, bringing out the unsuspected nobility of some, the strength of others, and in one case revealing an essentially comic aspect. He was a short, gingery, active man with a nose and chin of the Punch type, and whom his ship-mates called "Frenchy". I don't know why. He may have been a Frenchman, but I have never heard him utter a single word in French.

To see him coming aft to the wheel comforted one. The blue dungaree trousers turned up the calf, one leg a little higher than the other, the clean check shirt, the white canvas cap, evidently made by himself, made up a whole of peculiar smartness, and the persistent jauntiness of his gait, even, poor fellow, when he couldn't help tottering, told of his invincible spirit. There was also a man called Gambril.* He was the only grizzled person in the ship. His face was of an austere type. But if I remember all their faces, wasting tragically before my eyes, most of their names have vanished from my memory.

The words that passed between us were few and puerile in regard of the situation. I had to force myself to look them in the face. I expected to meet reproachful glances. There were none. The expression of suffering in their eyes was indeed hard enough to bear. But that they couldn't help. For the rest, I ask myself whether it was the temper of their souls or the sympathy of their imagination that made them so wonderful, so worthy of my undying regard.

For myself, neither my soul was highly tempered, nor my imagination properly under control. There were moments when I felt, not only that I would go mad, but that I had gone mad already; so that I dared not open my lips for fear of betraying myself by some insane shriek. Luckily I had only orders to give, and an order has a steadying influence upon him who has to give it. Moreover, the seaman, the officer of the watch, in me was sufficiently sane. I was like a mad carpenter making a box. Were he ever so convinced that he was King of Jerusalem, the box he would make would be a sane box. What I feared was a shrill note escaping me involuntarily and upsetting my balance. Luckily, again, there was no necessity to raise one's voice. The brooding stillness of the world seemed sensitive to the slightest sound like a whispering gallery. The conversational tone would almost carry a word from one end of the ship to the other. The terrible thing was that the only voice that I ever heard was my own. At night especially it reverberated very lonely amongst the planes of the unstirring sails.

Mr. Burns, still keeping to his bed with that air of secret determination, was moved to grumble at many things. Our interviews were short five-minute affairs, but fairly frequent. I was everlastingly diving down below to get a light, though I did not consume much tobacco at that time. The pipe was always going out; for in truth my mind was not composed enough to enable me to get a decent smoke. Likewise, for most of the time during the twenty-four hours I could have struck matches on deck and held them aloft till the flame burnt my fingers. But I always used to run below. It was a change. It was the only break in the incessant strain; and, of course, Mr. Burns through the open door could see me come in and go out every time.

With his knees gathered up under his chin and staring with his greenish eyes over them, he was a weird figure, and with my knowledge of the crazy notion in his head, not a very attractive one for me. Still, I had to speak to him now and then, and one day he complained that the ship was very silent. For hours and hours, he said,

he was lying there, not hearing a sound, till he did not
know what to do with himself.

"When Ransome happens to be forward in his
galley everything's so still that one might think everybody in the ship was dead," he grumbled. "The
only voice I do hear sometimes is yours, sir, and that
isn't enough to cheer me up. What's the matter with
the men? Isn't there one left that can sing out at the
ropes?"

"Not one, Mr. Burns," I said. "There is no breath
to spare on board this ship for that. Are you aware
that there are times when I can't muster more than
three hands to do anything?"

He asked swiftly but fearfully:

"Nobody dead yet, sir?"

"No."

"It wouldn't do," Mr. Burns declared forcibly.
"Mustn't let him. If he gets hold of one he will get
them all."

I cried out angrily at this. I believe I even swore
at the disturbing effect of these words. They attacked
all the self-possession that was left to me. In my endless vigil in the face of the enemy I had been haunted
by gruesome images enough. I had had visions of a
ship drifting in calms and swinging in light airs, with
all her crew dying slowly about her decks. Such things
had been known to happen.

Mr. Burns met my outburst by a mysterious silence.

"Look here," I said. "You don't believe yourself
what you say. You can't. It's impossible. It isn't
the sort of thing I have a right to expect from you.
My position's bad enough without being worried with
your silly fancies."

He remained unmoved. On account of the way in
which the light fell on his head I could not be sure

whether he had smiled faintly or not. I changed my tone.

"Listen," I said. "It's getting so desperate that I had thought for a moment, since we can't make our way south, whether I wouldn't try to steer west and make an attempt to reach the mail-boat track. We could always get some quinine from her, at least. What do you think?"

He cried out: "No, no, no. Don't do that, sir. You mustn't for a moment give up facing that old ruffian. If you do he will get the upper hand of us."

I left him. He was impossible. It was like a case of possession. His protest, however, was essentially quite sound. As a matter of fact, my notion of heading out west on the chance of sighting a problematical steamer could not bear calm examination. On the side where we were we had enough wind, at least from time to time, to struggle on towards the south. Enough, at least, to keep hope alive. But suppose that I had used those capricious gusts of wind to sail away to the westward, into some region where there was not a breath of air for days on end, what then? Perhaps my appalling vision of a ship floating with a dead crew would become a reality for the discovery weeks afterwards by some horror-stricken mariners.

That afternoon Ransome brought me up a cup of tea, and while waiting there, tray in hand, he remarked in the exactly right tone of sympathy:

"You are holding out well, sir."

"Yes," I said. "You and I seem to have been forgotten."

"Forgotten, sir?"

"Yes, by the fever-devil who has got on board this ship," I said.

Ransome gave me one of his attractive, intelligent,

quick glances and went away with the tray. It occurred to me that I had been talking somewhat in Mr.
Burns' manner. It annoyed me. Yet often in darker
moments I forgot myself into an attitude towards our
troubles more fit for a contest against a living enemy.

Yes. The fever-devil had not laid his hand yet
either on Ransome or on me. But he might at any
time. It was one of those thoughts one had to fight
down, keep at arm's length at any cost. It was unbear-
able to contemplate the possibility of Ransome, the
housekeeper of the ship, being laid low. And what
would happen to my command if I got knocked over,
with Mr. Burns too weak to stand without holding on
to his bed-place and the second mate reduced to a state
of permanent imbecility? It was impossible to imagine, or, rather, it was only too easy to imagine.

I was alone on the poop. The ship having no steerage way, I had sent the helmsman away to sit down or
lie down somewhere in the shade. The men's strength
was so reduced that all unnecessary calls on it had to
be avoided. It was the austere Gambril with the
grizzly beard. He went away readily enough, but he
was so weakened by repeated bouts of fever, poor
fellow, that in order to get down the poop ladder he
had to turn sideways and hang on with both hands
to the brass rail. It was just simply heart-breaking
to watch. Yet he was neither very much worse nor
much better than most of the half-dozen miserable
victims I could muster up on deck.

It was a terribly lifeless afternoon. For several
days in succession low clouds had appeared in the distance, white masses with dark convolutions resting on
the water, motionless, almost solid, and yet all the time
changing their aspects subtly. Towards evening they
vanished as a rule. But this day they awaited the

setting sun, which glowed and smouldered sulkily amongst them before it sank down. The punctual and wearisome stars reappeared over our mast-heads, but the air remained stagnant and oppressive.

The unfailing Ransome lighted the binnacle* lamps and glided, all shadowy, up to me.

"Will you go down and try to eat something, sir?" he suggested.

His low voice startled me. I had been standing looking out over the rail, saying nothing, feeling nothing, not even the weariness of my limbs, overcome by the evil spell.

"Ransome," I asked abruptly, "how long have I been on deck? I am losing the notion of time."

"Fourteen days, sir," he said. "It was a fortnight last Monday since we left the anchorage."

His equable voice sounded mournful somehow. He waited a bit, then added: "It's the first time that it looks as if we were to have some rain."

I noticed then the broad shadow on the horizon extinguishing the low stars completely, while those overhead, when I looked up, seemed to shine down on us through a veil of smoke.

How it got there, how it had crept up so high, I couldn't say. It had an ominous appearance. The air did not stir. At a renewed invitation from Ransome I did go down into the cabin to—in his words—"try and eat something." I don't know that the trial was very successful. I suppose at that period I did exist on food in the usual way; but the memory is now that in those days life was sustained on invincible anguish, as a sort of infernal stimulant exciting and consuming at the same time.

It's the only period of my life in which I attempted to keep a diary. No, not the only one. Years later,

in conditions of moral isolation, I did put down on
paper the thoughts and events of a score of days.
But this was the first time. I don't remember how it
came about or how the pocket-book and the pencil
came into my hands. It's inconceivable that I should
have looked for them on purpose. I suppose they
saved me from the crazy trick of talking to myself.

Strangely enough, in both cases I took to that sort
of thing in circumstances in which I did not expect, in
colloquial phrase, "to come out of it." Neither could
I expect the record to outlast me. This shows that it
was purely a personal need for intimate relief and not a
call of egotism.

Here I must give another sample of it, a few detached
lines, now looking very ghostly to my own eyes, out of
the part scribbled that very evening:—

*   *   *

There is something going on in the sky like a decomposition, like
a corruption of the air, which remains as still as ever. After all,
mere clouds, which may or may not hold wind or rain. Strange
that it should trouble me so. I feel as if all my sins had found me
out. But I suppose the trouble is that the ship is still lying motionless, not under command; and that I have nothing to do to keep
my imagination from running wild amongst the disastrous images
of the worst that may befall us. What's going to happen? Probably nothing. Or anything. It may be a furious squall coming,
butt-end foremost. And on deck there are five men with the
vitality and the strength of, say, two. We may have all our sails
blown away. Every stitch of canvas has been on her since we broke
ground at the mouth of the Mei-nam,* fifteen days ago . . . or
fifteen centuries. It seems to me that all my life before that
momentous day is infinitely remote, a fading memory of light-
hearted youth, something on the other side of a shadow. Yes, sails
may very well be blown away. And that would be like a death
sentence on the men. We haven't strength enough on board to
bend another suit; incredible thought, but it is true. Or we may
even get dismasted. Ships have been dismasted in squalls simply

because they weren't handled quick enough, and we have no power to whirl the yards around. It's like being bound hand and foot preparatory to having one's throat cut. And what appals me most of all is that I shrink from going on deck to face it. It's due to the ship, it's due to the men who are there on deck—some of them, ready to put out the last remnant of their strength at a word from me. And I am shrinking from it. From the mere vision. My first command. Now I understand that strange sense of insecurity in my past. I always suspected that I might be no good. And here is proof positive, I am shirking it, I am no good.

*   *   *

At that moment, or, perhaps, the moment after, I became aware of Ransome standing in the cabin. Something in his expression startled me. It had a meaning which I could not make out. I exclaimed:

"Somebody's dead."

It was his turn then to look startled.

"Dead? Not that I know of, sir. I have been in the forecastle only ten minutes ago and there was no dead man there then."

"You did give me a scare," I said.

His voice was extremely pleasant to listen to. He explained that he had come down below to close Mr. Burns' port in case it should come on to rain. He did not know that I was in the cabin, he added.

"How does it look outside?" I asked him.

"Very black indeed, sir. There is something in it for certain."

"In what quarter?"

"All round, sir."

I repeated idly: "All round. For certain," with my elbows on the table.

Ransome lingered in the cabin as if he had something to do there, but hesitated about doing it. I said suddenly:

"You think I ought to be on deck?"

He answered at once but without any particular emphasis or accent: "I do, sir."

I got to my feet briskly, and he made way for me to go out. As I passed through the lobby I heard Mr. Burns' voice saying:

"Shut the door of my room, will you, steward?" And Ransome's rather surprised: "Certainly, sir."

I thought that all my feelings had been dulled into complete indifference. But I found it as trying as ever to be on deck. The impenetrable blackness beset the ship so close that it seemed that by thrusting one's hand over the side one could touch some unearthly substance. There was in it an effect of inconceivable terror and of inexpressible mystery. The few stars overhead shed a dim light upon the ship alone, with no gleams of any kind upon the water, in detached shafts piercing an atmosphere which had turned to soot. It was something I had never seen before, giving no hint of the direction from which any change would come, the closing in of a menace from all sides.

There was still no man at the helm. The immobility of all things was perfect. If the air had turned black, the sea, for all I knew, might have turned solid. It was no good looking in any direction, watching for any sign, speculating upon the nearness of the moment. When the time came the blackness would overwhelm silently the bit of starlight falling upon the ship, and the end of all things would come without a sigh, stir, or murmur of any kind, and all our hearts would cease to beat like run-down clocks.

It was impossible to shake off that sense of finality. The quietness that came over me was like a foretaste of annihilation. It gave me a sort of comfort, as though my soul had become suddenly reconciled to an eternity of blind stillness.

The seaman's instinct alone survived whole in my moral dissolution. I descended the ladder to the quarter-deck. The starlight seemed to die out before reaching that spot, but when I asked quietly: "Are you there, men?" my eyes made out shadowy forms starting up around me, very few, very indistinct; and a voice spoke: "All here, sir." Another amended anxiously: "All that are any good for anything, sir."

Both voices were very quiet and unringing; without any special character of readiness or discouragement. Very matter-of-fact voices.

"We must try to haul this mainsail close up," I said.

The shadows swayed away from me without a word. Those men were the ghosts of themselves, and their weight on a rope could be no more than the weight of a bunch of ghosts. Indeed, if ever a sail was hauled up by sheer spiritual strength it must have been that sail, for, properly speaking, there was not muscle enough for the task in the whole ship, let alone the miserable lot of us on deck. Of course, I took the lead in the work myself. They wandered feebly after me from rope to rope, stumbling and panting. They toiled like Titans.* We were an hour at it at least, and all the time the black universe made no sound. When the last leech-line* was made fast, my eyes, accustomed to the darkness, made out the shapes of exhausted men drooping over the rails, collapsed on hatches. One hung over the after-capstan, sobbing for breath; and I stood amongst them like a tower of strength, impervious to disease and feeling only the sickness of my soul. I waited for some time fighting against the weight of my sins, against my sense of unworthiness, and then I said:

"Now, men, we'll go aft and square the mainyard. That's about all we can do for the ship; and for the rest she must take her chance."

VI

As we all went up it occurred to me that there ought
to be a man at the helm. I raised my voice not much
above a whisper, and, noiselessly, an uncomplaining
spirit in a fever-wasted body appeared in the light aft,
the head with hollow eyes illuminated against the
blackness which had swallowed up our world—and
the universe. The bare fore-arm extended over the
upper spokes seemed to shine with a light of its own.
I murmured to that luminous appearance:

"Keep the helm right amidships."

It answered in a tone of patient suffering:

"Right amidships, sir."

Then I descended to the quarter-deck. It was impossible to tell whence the blow would come. To
look round the ship was to look into a bottomless,
black pit. The eye lost itself in inconceivable depths.
I wanted to ascertain whether the ropes had been
picked up off the deck. One could only do that by feeling with one's feet. In my cautious progress I came
against a man in whom I recognized Ransome. He
possessed an unimpaired physical solidity which was
manifest to me at the contact. He was leaning against
the quarter-deck capstan and kept silent. It was like
a revelation. He was the collapsed figure sobbing
for breath I had noticed before we went on the
poop.

"You have been helping with the mainsail!" I exclaimed in a low tone.

"Yes, sir," sounded his quiet voice.

"Man! What were you thinking of? You mustn't do that sort of thing."

After a pause he assented. "I suppose I mustn't." Then after another short silence he added: "I am all right now," quickly, between the tell-tale gasps.

I could neither hear nor see anybody else; but when I spoke up, answering sad murmurs filled the quarter-deck, and its shadows seemed to shift here and there. I ordered all the halyards laid down on deck clear for running.

"I'll see to that, sir," volunteered Ransome in his natural, pleasant tone, which comforted one and aroused one's compassion too, somehow.

That man ought to have been in his bed, resting, and my plain duty was to send him there. But perhaps he would not have obeyed me. I had not the strength of mind to try. All I said was:

"Go about it quietly, Ransome."

Returning on the poop I approached Gambril. His face, set with hollow shadows in the light, looked awful, finally silenced. I asked him how he felt, but hardly expected an answer. Therefore I was astonished at his comparative loquacity.

"Them shakes leaves me as weak as a kitten, sir," he said, preserving finely that air of unconsciousness as to anything but his business a helmsman should never lose. "And before I can pick up my strength that there hot fit comes along and knocks me over again."

He sighed. There was no complaint in his tone, but the bare words were enough to give me a horrible pang of self-reproach. It held me dumb for a time. When the tormenting sensation had passed off I asked:

"Do you feel strong enough to prevent the rudder taking charge if she gets sternway on her? It wouldn't do to get something smashed about the steering-gear now. We've enough difficulties to cope with as it is."

He answered with just a shade of weariness that he was strong enough to hang on. He could promise me that she shouldn't take the wheel out of his hands. More he couldn't say.

, At that moment Ransome appeared quite close to me, stepping out of the darkness into visibility suddenly, as if just created with his composed face and pleasant voice.

Every rope on deck, he said, was laid down clear for running, as far as one could make certain by feeling. It was impossible to see anything. Frenchy had stationed himself forward. He said he had a jump or two left in him yet.

Here a faint smile altered for an instant the clear, firm design of Ransome's lips. With his serious, clear, grey eyes, his serene temperament, he was a priceless man altogether. Soul as firm as the muscles of his body.

He was the only man on board (except me, but I had to preserve my liberty of movement) who had a sufficiency of muscular strength to trust to. For a moment I thought I had better ask him to take the wheel. But the dreadful knowledge of the enemy he had to carry about him made me hesitate. In my ignorance of physiology it occurred to me that he might die suddenly, from excitement, at a critical moment.

While this gruesome fear restrained the ready words on the tip of my tongue, Ransome stepped back two paces and vanished from my sight.

At once an uneasiness possessed me, as if some support had been withdrawn. I moved forward too, outside the circle of light, into the darkness that stood in front of me like a wall. In one stride I penetrated it.

Such must have been the darkness before creation. It had closed behind me. I knew I was invisible to the man at the helm. Neither could I see anything. He was alone, I was alone, every man was alone where he stood. And every form was gone, too, spar, sail, fittings, rails; everything was blotted out in the dreadful smoothness of that absolute night.

A flash of lightning would have been a relief—I mean physically. I would have prayed for it if it hadn't been for my shrinking apprehension of the thunder. In the tension of silence I was suffering from it seemed to me that the first crash must turn me into dust.

And thunder was, most likely, what would happen next. Stiff all over and hardly breathing, I waited with a horribly strained expectation. Nothing happened. It was maddening. But a dull, growing ache in the lower part of my face made me aware that I had been grinding my teeth madly enough, for God knows how long.

It's extraordinary I should not have heard myself doing it; but I hadn't. By an effort which absorbed all my faculties I managed to keep my jaw still. It required much attention, and while thus engaged I became bothered by curious, irregular sounds of faint tapping on the deck. They could be heard single, in pairs, in groups. While I wondered at this mysterious devilry, I received a slight blow under the left eye and felt an enormous tear run down my cheek. Raindrops. Enormous. Forerunners of something. Tap. Tap. Tap . . . .

I turned about, and, addressing Gambril earnestly, entreated him to "hang on to the wheel." But I could hardly speak from emotion. The fatal moment had come. I held my breath. The tapping had stopped as unexpectedly as it had begun, and there was a renewed moment of intolerable suspense; something like an additional turn of the racking screw. I don't suppose I would have ever screamed, but I remember my conviction that there was nothing else for it but to scream.

Suddenly—how am I to convey it? Well, suddenly the darkness turned into water. This is the only suitable figure. A heavy shower, a downpour, comes along, making a noise. You hear its approach on the sea, in the air too, I verily believe. But this was different. With no preliminary whisper or rustle, without a splash, and even without the ghost of impact, I became instantaneously soaked to the skin. Not a very difficult matter, since I was wearing only my sleeping suit.* My hair got full of water in an instant, water streamed on my skin, it filled my nose, my ears, my eyes. In a fraction of a second I swallowed quite a lot of it.

As to Gambril, he was fairly choked. He coughed pitifully, the broken cough of a sick man; and I beheld him as one sees a fish in an aquarium by the light of an electric bulb, an elusive, phosphorescent shape. Only he did not glide away. But something else happened. Both binnacle lamps went out. I suppose the water forced itself into them, though I wouldn't have thought that possible, for they fitted into the cowl perfectly.

The last gleam of light in the universe had gone, pursued by a low exclamation of dismay from Gambril. I groped for him and seized his arm. How startlingly wasted it was.

"Never mind," I said. "You don't want the light. All you need to do is to keep the wind, when it comes, at the back of your head. You understand?"

"Aye, aye, sir. . . . But I should like to have a light," he added nervously.

Áll that time the ship lay as steady as a rock. The noise of the water pouring off the sails and spars, flowing over the break of the poop, had stopped short. The poop scuppers* gurgled and sobbed for a little while longer, and then perfect silence, joined to perfect immobility, proclaimed the yet unbroken spell of our helplessness, poised on the edge of some violent issue, lurking in the dark.

I started forward restlessly. I did not need my sight to pace the poop of my ill-starred first command with perfect assurance. Every square foot of her decks was impressed indelibly on my brain, to the very grain and knots of the planks. Yet, all of a sudden, I fell clean over something, landing full length on my hands and face.

It was something big and alive. Not a dog—more like a sheep, rather. But there were no animals in the ship. How could an animal. . . . It was an added and fantastic horror which I could not resist. The hair of my head stirred even as I picked myself up, awfully scared; not as a man is scared while his judgment, his reason still try to resist, but completely, boundlessly, and, as it were, innocently scared—like a little child.

I could see It—that Thing! The darkness, of which so much had just turned into water, had thinned down a little. There It was! But I did not hit upon the notion of Mr. Burns issuing out of the companion on all fours till he attempted to stand up, and even then the idea of a bear crossed my mind first.

He growled like one when I seized him round the body. He had buttoned himself up into an enormous winter overcoat of some woolly material, the weight of which was too much for his reduced state. I could hardly feel the incredibly thin lath of his body, lost within the thick stuff, but his growl had depth and substance: Confounded dumb ship with a craven, tip-toeing crowd. Why couldn't they stamp and go with a brace? Wasn't there one God-forsaken lubber* in the lot fit to raise a yell on a rope?

"Skulking's no good, sir," he attacked me directly. "You can't slink past the old murderous ruffian. It isn't the way. You must go for him boldly—as I did. Boldness is what you want. Show him that you don't care for any of his damned tricks. Kick up a jolly old row."

"Good God, Mr. Burns," I said angrily. "What on earth are you up to? What do you mean by coming up on deck in this state?"

"Just that! Boldness. The only way to scare the old bullying rascal."

I pushed him, still growling, against the rail. "Hold on to it," I said roughly. I did not know what to do with him. I left him in a hurry, to go to Gambril, who had called faintly that he believed there was some wind aloft. Indeed, my own ears had caught a feeble flutter of wet canvas, high up overhead, the jingle of a slack chain sheet. . . .

These were eerie, disturbing, alarming sounds in the dead stillness of the air around me. All the instances I had heard of topmasts being whipped out of a ship while there was not wind enough on her deck to blow out a match rushed into my memory.

"I can't see the upper sails, sir," declared Gambril shakily.

"Don't move the helm. You'll be all right," I said confidently.

The poor man's nerve was gone. I was not in much better case. It was the moment of breaking strain and was relieved by the abrupt sensation of the ship moving forward as if of herself under my feet. I heard plainly the soughing of the wind aloft, the low cracks of the upper spars taking the strain, long before I could feel the least draught on my face turned aft, anxious and sightless like the face of a blind man.

Suddenly a louder sounding note filled our ears, the darkness started streaming against our bodies, chilling them exceedingly. Both of us, Gambril and I, shivered violently in our clinging, soaked garments of thin cotton. I said to him:

"You are all right now, my man. All you've got to do is to keep the wind at the back of your head. Surely you are up to that. A child could steer this ship in smooth water."

He muttered: "Aye! A healthy child." And I felt ashamed of having been passed over by the fever which had been preying on every man's strength but mine, in order that my remorse might be the more bitter, the feeling of unworthiness more poignant, and the sense of responsibility heavier to bear.

The ship had gathered great way on her almost at once on the calm water. I felt her slipping through it with no other noise but a mysterious rustle alongside. Otherwise she had no motion at all, neither lift nor roll. It was a disheartening steadiness which had lasted for eighteen days now; for never, never had we had wind enough in that time to raise the slightest run of the sea. The breeze freshened suddenly. I thought it was high time to get Mr. Burns off the deck. He worried me. I looked upon him as a lunatic who would be very likely to start roaming over the ship and break a limb or fall overboard.

I was truly glad to find he had remained holding on where I had left him, sensibly enough. He was, however, muttering to himself ominously.

This was discouraging. I remarked in a matter-of-fact tone:

"We have never had so much wind as this since we left the roads."

"There's some heart in it too," he growled judiciously. It was a remark of a perfectly sane seaman. But he added immediately: "It was about time I should come on deck. I've been nursing my strength for this— just for this. Do you see it, sir?"

I said I did, and proceeded to hint that it would be advisable for him to go below now and take a rest.

His answer was an indignant: "Go below! Not if I know it, sir."

Very cheerful! He was a horrible nuisance. And all at once he started to argue. I could feel his crazy excitement in the dark.

"You don't know how to go about it, sir. How could you? All this whispering and tip-toeing is no good. You can't hope to slink past a cunning, wide-awake, evil brute like he was. You never heard him talk. Enough to make your hair stand on end. No! No! He wasn't mad. He was no more mad than I am. He was just downright wicked. Wicked so as to frighten most people. I will tell you what he was. He was nothing less than a thief and a murderer at heart. And do you think he's any different now because he's dead? Not he! His carcass lies a hundred fathom under, but he's just the same . . . in latitude 8° 20′ North."

He snorted defiantly. I noted with weary resignation that the breeze had got lighter while he raved. He was at it again.

"I ought to have thrown the beggar out of the ship over the rail like a dog. It was only on account of the

men. . . . Fancy having to read the Burial Service
over a brute like that! . . . 'Our departed brother'
. . . I could have laughed. That was what he
couldn't bear. I suppose I am the only man that ever
stood up to laugh at him. When he got sick it used to
scare that . . . brother . . . Brother . . .* Departed . . . Sooner call a shark brother."

The breeze had let go so suddenly that the way of
the ship brought the wet sails heavily against the mast.
The spell of deadly stillness had caught us up again.
There seemed to be no escape.

"Hallo!" exclaimed Mr. Burns in a startled voice.
"Calm again!"

I addressed him as though he had been sane.

"This is the sort of thing we've been having for seventeen days, Mr. Burns," I said with intense bitterness.
"A puff, then a calm, and in a moment, you'll see, she'll
be swinging on her heel with her head away from her
course to the devil somewhere."

He caught at the word. "The old dodging Devil,"
he screamed piercingly, and burst into such a loud
laugh as I had never heard before. It was a provoking,
mocking peal, with a hair-raising, screeching over-note
of defiance. I stepped back utterly confounded.

Instantly there was a stir on the quarter-deck, murmurs of dismay. A distressed voice cried out in the
dark below us: "Who's that gone crazy, now?"

Perhaps they thought it was their captain! Rush
is not the word that could be applied to the utmost
speed the poor fellows were up to; but in an amazing
short time every man in the ship able to walk upright
had found his way on to that poop.

I shouted to them: "It's the mate. Lay hold of him
a couple of you. . . ."

I expected this performance to end in a ghastly sort

of fight. But Mr. Burns cut his derisive screeching dead short and turned upon them fiercely, yelling:

"Aha! Dog-gone ye! You've found your tongues —have ye? I thought you were dumb.. Well, then— laugh! Laugh—I tell you. Now then—all together. One, two, three—laugh!"

A moment of silence ensued, of silence so profound that you could have heard a pin drop on the deck. Then Ransome's unperturbed voice uttered pleasantly the words:

"I think he has fainted, sir——" The little motionless knot of men stirred, with low murmurs of relief. "I've got him under the arms. Get hold of his legs, someone."

Yes. It was a relief. He was silenced for a time— for a time. I could not have stood another peal of that insane screeching. I was sure of it; and just then Gambril, the austere Gambril, treated us to another vocal performance. He began to sing out for relief. His voice wailed pitifully in the darkness: "Come aft, somebody! I can't stand this. Here she'll be off again directly and I can't. . . ."

I dashed aft myself meeting on my way a hard gust of wind whose approach Gambril's ear had detected from afar and which filled the sails on the main in a series of muffled reports mingled with the low plaint of the spars. I was just in time to. seize the wheel while Frenchy, who had followed me, caught up the collapsing Gambril. He hauled him out of the way, admonished him to lie still where he was, and then stepped up to relieve me, asking calmly:

"How am I to steer her, sir?"

"Dead before it, for the present. I'll get you a light in a moment."

But going forward I met Ransome bringing up the

spare binnacle lamp. That man noticed everything, attended to everything, shed comfort around him as he moved. As he passed me he remarked in a soothing tone that the stars were coming out. They were. The breeze was sweeping clear the sooty sky, breaking through the indolent silence of the sea.

The barrier of awful stillness which had encompassed us for so many days as though we had been accursed was broken. I felt that. I let myself fall on to the skylight seat. A faint white ridge of foam, thin, very thin, broke alongside. The first for ages—for ages. I could have cheered, if it hadn't been for the sense of guilt which clung to all my thoughts secretly. Ransome stood before me.

"What about the mate," I asked anxiously. "Still unconscious?"

"Well, sir—it's funny." Ransome was evidently puzzled. "He hasn't spoken a word, and his eyes are shut. But it looks to me more like sound sleep than anything else."

I accepted this view as the least troublesome of any, or at any rate, least disturbing. Dead faint or deep slumber, Mr. Burns had to be left to himself for the present. Ransome remarked suddenly:

"I believe you want a coat, sir."

"I believe I do," I sighed out.

But I did not move. What I felt I wanted were new limbs. My arms and legs seemed utterly useless, fairly worn out. They didn't even ache. But I stood up all the same to put on the coat when Ransome brought it up. And when he suggested that he had better now "take Gambril forward," I said:

"All right. I'll help you to get him down on the main deck."

I found that I was quite able to help, too. We

raised Gambril up between us. He tried to help himself along like a man, but all the time he was inquiring piteously:

"You won't let me go when we come to the ladder? You won't let me go when we come to the ladder?"

The breeze kept on freshening and blew true, true to a hair. At daylight by careful manipulation of the helm we got the foreyards to run square by themselves (the water keeping smooth) and then went about hauling the ropes tight. Of the four men I had with me at night, I could see now only two. I didn't inquire as to the others. They had given in. For a time only I hoped.

Our various tasks forward occupied us for hours, the two men with me moved so slowly and had to rest so often. One of them remarked that "every blamed thing in the ship felt about a hundred times heavier than its proper weight." This was the only complaint uttered. I don't know what we should have done without Ransome. He worked with us, silent too, with a little smile frozen on his lips. From time to time I murmured to him: "Go steady"—"Take it easy, Ransome"—and received a quick glance in reply.

When we had done all we could do to make things safe, he disappeared into his galley. Some time afterwards, going forward for a look round, I caught sight of him through the open door. He sat upright on the locker in front of the stove, with his head leaning back against the bulkhead. His eyes were closed; his capable hands held open the front of his thin cotton shirt baring tragically his powerful chest, which heaved in painful and laboured gasps. He didn't hear me.

I retreated quietly and went straight on to the poop

to relieve Frenchy, who by that time was beginning to look very sick. He gave me the course with great formality and tried to go off with a jaunty step, but reeled widely twice before getting out of my sight.

And then I remained all alone aft, steering my ship, which ran before the wind with a buoyant lift now and then, and even rolling a little. Presently Ransome appeared before me with a tray. The sight of food made me ravenous all at once. He took the wheel while I sat down on the after grating to eat my breakfast.

"This breeze seems to have done for our crowd," he murmured. "It just laid them low—all hands."

"Yes," I said. "I suppose you and I are the only two fit men in the ship."

"Frenchy says there's still a jump left in him. I don't know. It can't be much," continued Ransome with his wistful smile. "Good little man that. But suppose, sir, that this wind flies round when we are close to the land—what are we going to do with her?"

"If the wind shifts round heavily after we close in with the land she will either run ashore or get dismasted or both. We won't be able to do anything with her. She's running away with us now. All we can do is to steer her. She's a ship without a crew."

"Yes. All laid low," repeated Ransome quietly. "I do give them a look-in forward every now and then, but it's precious little I can do for them."

"I, and the ship, and everyone on board of her, are very much indebted to you, Ransome," I said warmly.

He made as though he had not heard me, and steered in silence till I was ready to relieve him. He surrendered the wheel, picked up the tray, and for a parting shot informed me that Mr. Burns was awake and seemed to have a mind to come up on deck.

"I don't know how to prevent him, sir. I can't very well stop down below all the time."

It was clear that he couldn't. And sure enough Mr. Burns came on deck dragging himself painfully aft in his enormous overcoat. I beheld him with a natural dread. To have him around and raving about the wiles of a dead man while I had to steer a wildly rushing ship full of dying men was a rather dreadful prospect.

But his first remarks were quite sensible in meaning and tone. Apparently he had no recollection of the night scene. And if he had he didn't betray himself once. Neither did he talk very much. He sat on the skylight looking desperately ill at first, but that strong breeze, before which the last remnant of my crew had wilted down, seemed to blow a fresh stock of vigour into his frame with every gust. One could almost see the process.

By way of sanity test I alluded on purpose to the late captain. I was delighted to find that Mr. Burns did not display undue interest in the subject. He ran over the old tale of that savage ruffian's iniquities with a certain vindictive gusto and then concluded unexpectedly:

"I do believe, sir, that his brain began to go a year or more before he died."

A wonderful recovery. I could hardly spare it as much admiration as it deserved, for I had to give all my mind to the steering.

In comparison with the hopeless languor of the preceding days this was dizzy speed. Two ridges of foam streamed from the ship's bows; the wind sang in a strenuous note which under other circumstances would have expressed to me all the joy of life. Whenever the hauled-up mainsail started trying to slat*and bang itself to pieces in its gear, Mr. Burns would look at me apprehensively.

"What would you have me do, Mr. Burns? We can neither furl it nor set it. I only wish the old thing would thrash itself to pieces and be done with it. This beastly racket confuses me."

Mr. Burns wrung his hands, and cried out suddenly:

"How will you get the ship into harbour, sir, without men to handle her?"

And I couldn't tell him.

Well—it did get done about forty hours afterwards. By the exorcising virtue of Mr. Burns' awful laugh, the malicious spectre had been laid, the evil spell broken, the curse removed. We were now in the hands of a kind and energetic Providence. It was rushing us on. . . .

I shall never forget the last night, dark, windy, and starry. I steered. Mr. Burns, after having obtained from me a solemn promise to give him a kick if anything happened, went frankly to sleep on the deck close to the binnacle. Convalescents need sleep. Ransome, his back propped against the mizzenmast and a blanket over his legs, remained perfectly still, but I don't suppose he closed his eyes for a moment. That embodiment of jauntiness, Frenchy, still under the delusion that there was "a jump" left in him, had insisted on joining us; but mindful of discipline, had laid himself down as far on the forepart of the poop as he could get, alongside the bucket-rack.

And I steered, too tired for anxiety, too tired for connected thought. I had moments of grim exultation and then my heart would sink awfully at the thought of that forecastle at the other end of the dark

deck, full of fever-stricken men—some of them dying.
By my fault. But never mind. Remorse must wait.
I had to steer.

In the small hours the breeze weakened, then failed
altogether. About five it returned, gentle enough,
enabling us to head for the roadstead. Daybreak
found Mr. Burns sitting wedged up with coils of rope
on the stern-grating, and from the depths of his overcoat steering the ship with very white bony hands; while
Ransome and I rushed along the decks letting go all
the sheets and halliards* by the run. We dashed next
up on to the forecastle head. The perspiration of labour
and sheer nervousness simply poured off our heads
as we toiled to get the anchors cock-billed.* I dared
not look at Ransome as we worked side by side. We
exchanged curt words; I could hear him panting close
to me and I avoided turning my eyes his way for fear
of seeing him fall down and expire in the act of putting
out his strength—for what? Indeed for some distinct
ideal.

The consummate seaman in him was aroused. He
needed no directions. He knew what to do. Every
effort, every movement was an act of consistent heroism.
It was not for me to look at a man thus inspired.

At last all was ready, and I heard him say, "Hadn't
I better go down and open the compressors now, sir?"

"Yes. Do," I said. And even then I did not glance
his way. After a time his voice came up from the main
deck:

"When you like, sir. All clear on the windlass
here."

I made a sign to Mr. Burns to put the helm down
and then I let both anchors go one after another, leaving the ship to take as much cable as she wanted. She
took the best part of them both before she brought up.

The loose sails coming aback ceased their maddening racket above my head. A perfect stillness reigned in the ship. And while I stood forward feeling a little giddy in that sudden peace, I caught faintly a moan or two and the incoherent mutterings of the sick in the forecastle.

As we had a signal for medical assistance flying on the mizzen it is a fact that before the ship was fairly at rest three steam-launches from various men-of-war arrived alongside; and at least five naval surgeons clambered on board. They stood in a knot gazing up and down the empty main deck, then looked aloft—where not a man could be seen either.

I went towards them—a solitary figure in a blue and grey striped sleeping suit and a pipe-clayed cork helmet on its head. Their disgust was extreme. They had expected surgical cases. Each one had brought his carving tools with him. But they soon got over their little disappointment. In less than five minutes one of the steam-launches was rushing shorewards to order a big boat and some hospital people for the removal of the crew. The big steam-pinnace went off to her ship to bring over a few bluejackets*to furl my sails for me.

One of the surgeons had remained on board. He came out of the forecastle looking impenetrable, and noticed my inquiring gaze.

"There's nobody dead in there, if that's what you want to know," he said deliberately. Then added in a tone of wonder: "The whole crew!"

"And very bad?"

"And very bad," he repeated. His eyes were roaming all over the ship. "Heavens! What's that?"

"That," I said, glancing aft, "is Mr. Burns, my chief officer."

Mr. Burns with his moribund head nodding on the stalk of his lean neck was a sight for any one to exclaim at. The surgeon asked:

"Is he going to the hospital too?"

"Oh, no," I said jocosely. "Mr. Burns can't go on shore till the mainmast goes. I am very proud of him. He's my only convalescent."

"You look . . ." began the doctor staring at me. But I interrupted him angrily:

"I am not ill."

"No. . . . You look queer."

"Well, you see, I have been seventeen days on deck."

"Seventeen! . . . But you must have slept."

"I suppose I must have. I don't know. But I'm certain that I didn't sleep for the last forty hours."

"Phew! . . . You will be going ashore presently, I suppose?"

"As soon as ever I can. There's no end of business waiting for me there."

The surgeon released my hand, which he had taken while we talked, pulled out his pocket-book, wrote in it rapidly, tore out the page, and offered it to me.

"I strongly advise you to get this prescription made up for yourself ashore. Unless I am much mistaken you will need it this evening."

"What is it then?" I asked with suspicion.

"Sleeping draught," answered the surgeon curtly; and moving with an air of interest towards Mr. Burns he engaged him in conversation.

As I went below to dress to go ashore, Ransome followed me. He begged my pardon; he wished, too, to be sent ashore and paid off.

I looked at him in surprise. He was waiting for my answer with an air of anxiety.

"You don't mean to leave the ship!" I cried out.

"I do really, sir. I want to go and be quiet somewhere. Anywhere. The hospital will do."

"But, Ransome," I said, "I hate the idea of parting with you."

"I must go," he broke in. "I have a right!" He gasped and a look of almost savage determination passed over his face. For an instant he was another being. And I saw under the worth and the comeliness of the man the humble reality of things. Life was a boon to him—this precarious hard life—and he was thoroughly alarmed about himself.

"Of course I shall pay you off if you wish it," I hastened to say. "Only I must ask you to remain on board till this afternoon. I can't leave Mr. Burns absolutely by himself in the ship for hours."

He softened at once and assured me with a smile and in his natural pleasant voice that he understood that very well.

When I returned on deck everything was ready for the removal of the men. It was the last ordeal of that episode which had been maturing and tempering my character—though I did not know it.

It was awful. They passed under my eyes one after another—each of them an embodied reproach of the bitterest kind, till I felt a sort of revolt wake up in me. Poor Frenchy had gone suddenly under. He was carried past me insensible, his comic face horribly flushed and as if swollen, breathing stertorously. He looked more like Mr. Punch than ever; a disgracefully intoxicated Mr. Punch.

The austere Gambril, on the contrary, had improved temporarily. He insisted on walking on his own feet to the rail—of course with assistance on each side of him. But he gave way to a sudden panic at the moment of being swung over the side and began to wail pitifully:

"Don't let them drop me, sir. Don't let them drop me, sir!" While I kept on shouting to him in most soothing accents: "All right, Gambril. They won't! They won't!"

It was no doubt very ridiculous. The bluejackets on our deck were grinning quietly, while even Ransome himself (much to the fore in lending a hand) had to enlarge his wistful smile for a fleeting moment.

I left for the shore in the steam-pinnace, and on looking back beheld Mr. Burns actually standing up by the taffrail, still in his enormous woolly overcoat. The bright sunlight brought out his weirdness amazingly. He looked like a frightful and elaborate scarecrow set up on the poop of a death-stricken ship, to keep the seabirds from the corpses.

Our story had got about already in town and everybody on shore was most kind. The marine office let me off the port dues, and as there happened to be a shipwrecked crew staying in the Home I had no difficulty in obtaining as many men as I wanted. But when I inquired if I could see Captain Ellis for a moment I was told in accents of pity for my ignorance that our deputy-Neptune had retired and gone home on a pension about three weeks after I left the port. So I suppose that my appointment was the last act, outside the daily routine, of his official life.

It is strange how on coming ashore I was struck by the springy step, the lively eyes, the strong vitality of everyone I met. It impressed me enormously. And amongst those I met there was Captain Giles of course. It would have been very extraordinary if I had not met him. A prolonged stroll in the business part of the town was the regular employment of all his mornings when he was ashore.

I caught the glitter of the gold watch-chain across

his chest ever so far away. He radiated benevolence.

"What is it I hear?" he queried with a "kind uncle" smile, after shaking hands. "Twenty-one days from Bankok?"

"Is this all you've heard?" I said. "You must come to tiffin with me. I want you to know exactly what you have let me in for."

He hesitated for almost a minute.

"Well—I will," he decided condescendingly at last.

We turned into the hotel. I found to my surprise that I could eat quite a lot. Then over the cleared table-cloth I unfolded to Captain Giles all the story since I took command in all its professional and emotional aspects, while he smoked patiently the big cigar I had given him.

Then he observed sagely:

"You must feel jolly well tired by this time."

"No," I said. "Not tired. But I'll tell you, Captain Giles, how I feel. I feel old. And I must be. All of you on shore look to me just a lot of skittish youngsters that have never known a care in the world."

He didn't smile. He looked insufferably exemplary. He declared:

"That will pass. But you do look older—it's a fact."

"Aha!" I said.

"No! No! The truth is that one must not make too much of anything in life, good or bad."

"Live at half-speed," I murmured perversely. "Not everybody can do that."

"You'll be glad enough presently if you can keep going even at that rate," he retorted with his air of conscious virtue. "And there's another thing: a man should stand up to his bad luck, to his mistakes, to his conscience, and all that sort of thing. Why—what else would you have to fight against?"

I kept silent. I don't know what he saw in my face, but he asked abruptly:

"Why—you aren't faint-hearted?"

"God only knows, Captain Giles," was my sincere answer.

"That's all right," he said calmly. "You will learn soon how not to be faint-hearted. A man has got to learn everything—and that's what so many of those youngsters don't understand."

"Well I am no longer a youngster."

"No," he conceded. "Are you leaving soon?"

"I am going on board directly," I said. "I shall pick up one of my anchors and heave in to half-cable on the other as soon as my new crew comes on board and I shall be off at daylight to-morrow."

"You will?" grunted Captain Giles approvingly. "That's the way. You'll do."

"What did you expect? That I would want to take a week ashore for a rest?" I said, irritated by his tone. "There's no rest for me till she's out in the Indian Ocean and not much of it even then."

He puffed at the cigar moodily, as if transformed.

"Yes, that's what it amounts to," he said in a musing tone. It was as if a ponderous curtain had rolled up disclosing an unexpected Captain Giles. But it was only for a moment, merely the time to let him add: "Precious little rest in life for anybody. Better not think of it."

We rose, left the hotel, and parted from each other in the street with a warm handshake, just as he began to interest me for the first time in our intercourse.

The first thing I saw when I got back to the ship was

Ransome on the quarter-deck sitting quietly on his neatly lashed sea-chest.

I beckoned him to follow me into the saloon where I sat down to write a letter of recommendation for him to a man I knew on shore.

When finished I pushed it across the table. "It may be of some good to you when you leave the hospital."

He took it, put it in his pocket. His eyes were looking away from me—nowhere. His face was anxiously set.

"How are you feeling now?" I asked.

"I don't feel bad now, sir," he answered stiffly. "But I am afraid of its coming on. . . ." The wistful smile came back on his lips for a moment. "I—I am in a blue funk about my heart, sir."

I approached him with extended hand. His eyes, not looking at me, had a strained expression. He was like a man listening for a warning call.

"Won't you shake hands, Ransome?" I said gently.

He exclaimed, flushed up dusky red, gave my hand a hard wrench—and next moment, left alone in the cabin, I listened to him going up the companion stairs cautiously, step by step, in mortal fear of starting into sudden anger our common enemy it was his hard fate to carry consciously within his faithful breast.

THE END

EXPLANATORY NOTES

'Author's Note'

xxxix *the last three months of the year 1916*: a mistake on Conrad's part: the final page of his manuscript is dated 15 December 1915, and Jocelyn Baines refers to letters written by Conrad testifying to his having started writing the work in early 1915 (*Joseph Conrad: A Critical Biography*, Harmondsworth, Penguin, reprinted 1971, p. 485).

Text of The Shadow-Line

3 —*D'autres fois, calme plat, grand miroir/De mon désespoir*: the quotation from Baudelaire is from the sonnet 'La Musique' in *Les Fleurs du Mal*. It should end with an exclamation mark rather than a full stop.

    undiscovered country: an echo from *Hamlet*, III. i; the undiscovered country Hamlet is referring to is death.

4 *Red Ensign*: the flag of the British Merchant Marine.

    taffrail: from tafferel, the aftermost portion of the poop-rail of a ship; the poop is the aftermost (i.e., rear, or stern) part of the deck—often the highest deck.

    Syed: from the Arabic word for 'Lord': a Muslim honorary title, sometimes carrying the specific claim that the bearer is descended from Mohammed's grandson, Husain.

5 *Archipelago*: a sheet of water studded with numerous islands; here, specifically the Malay Archipelago.

    green sickness of late youth: 'green' can have the meanings 'immature', 'jealous', or 'vigorous'. The first is probably meant here.

    Kalashes: compare the following from Conrad's *Youth*: 'Four Calashes pulled a swinging stroke. This was my first sight of Malay seamen.'

6 *mist of fluffy brown beard*: a good example of Conrad's polishing of the text. The manuscript version reads, 'with a short fluffy brown beard all round his rather haggard face'.

dyspeptic: subject to indigestion.

7 *punkah*: a fan, or the servant who operates it.

Hades: in Greek mythology the underworld abode of the dead. The association between signing on or off for a voyage and being ferried across the river Styx to Hades is effectively used by Conrad at the start of *Heart of Darkness*.

8 *clinging to my rebellious discontent*: in Conrad's manuscript, 'clinging close to my discontented soul'.

9 *milliner*: a person (normally female) who makes up female articles of dress.

East End of London: at this time the poor or working-class quarter of London.

antimacassars: macassar oil was used as a hair-dressing. To prevent it from staining chairs, cloths covering the backs of chairs were used, hence antimacassar.

11 *Solo Sea trip*: Solo is now known as Surakarta, a river in central Java. It runs into the Solo Sea.

tiffin time: tiffin is a light midday meal.

12 *Palawan*: in the present-day Philippines.

14 *Rajah*: here a Malay or Java dignitary or ruler.

15 *siesta*: literally 'sixth hour': a nap or rest taken at midday.

16 *Queen Victoria's first jubilee celebrations*: in 1887.

19 *peon*: a native attendant or orderly.

25 *stuffy Philistinish lair*: Philistinish means 'without culture'.

that force somewhere within our lives which shapes them this way or that: another echo from *Hamlet*; see V. ii.

28 *this stale, unprofitable world of my discontent*: compare, again, *Hamlet*, II. ii.

29 *coxswain*: helmsman.

quill-driver: a quill is a pen, hence a derogatory term for a clerk.

30 *roadstead*: a place where ships may anchor near shore.

31 *deputy-Neptune*: Neptune was the Roman god of the sea, traditionally depicted holding a trident.

the official pen, far mightier than the sword: echoes the proverb 'The pen is mightier than the sword'—written documents are more powerful than physical force. The theme is a very common one in Conrad's writing.

Consul-General: an agent appointed by a sovereign state (here Britain) to protect the interests of citizens and to assist in commercial relations in a foreign country.

32 *Bankok*: nowadays normally spelled Bangkok, as it is in the 1921 Heinemann edition. The capital of modern Thailand.

In reality . . . getting up: cf. what we learn about this act on page 130.

34 *aureole*: a halo of radiating light—here used metaphorically and ironically.

man of pen and ink: the contrasting of this man with the men 'who grapple with realities outside' touches on a favourite theme of Conrad's.

37 *not to be surprised*: the 'not' was added by Conrad after the manuscript stage, suggesting that Conrad's second thoughts attributed rather different characteristics to youth.

41 *coolies*: hired native labourers.

42 *everybody in the world is a little mad*: this and other references to lunacy fit in well with the repeated echoes of *Hamlet*.

45 *stern-sheets*: the well of a small boat.

deepest slumber: in Conrad's manuscript the following passage, not to be found in the published version, follows at this point: 'deepest slumber—it receded still and soundless like a shadow in the hot night. And the anchored ships we passed one after another were as still and silent as if all the crews were dead. They were like tombs each with the unwinking light of a lantern above their dark solid shapes scattered on the polished level of the roadstead catching here and there the dim gleam of a star. The hail . . .'

47 *we crossed the bar*: crossed the bar of sand outside a harbour, in this instance to enter the harbour. The phrase can also be used to refer to the act of dying, and perhaps chimes with the earlier reference to Hades (p. 7).

the Oriental capital: Ban(g)kok, capital of Siam—modern Thailand.

49 *there she was*: in Conrad's manuscript the passage continues: 'Her lines her rigging filled my eye with a great content. And as you looked that feeling of the emptiness which had made me

discontented for the last few month [*sic*] of my life, that half conscious sense that existence is but a road to [??] death, lost its bitter plausibility, its evil influence dissolved in a sort of joyous emotion.'

50 *baulk*: a wooden beam.

  awning: part of a deck covered with a roof (often of canvas).

51 *companion-way*: staircase to cabin.

  lobby: an apartment normally adjacent to the cabin bulkhead (the upright partition dividing a hold or forming a part of a cabin).

52 *ormolu*: gold, or gold-coloured alloy.

53 *bulkheads*: see note for *lobby*, page 51.

55 *dégagé*: detached.

  '*I suppose she can travel—what?*': a reminder that the captain uses the idioms of an upper-class Englishman!

57 *seven bells in the forenoon watch*: during each watch a bell is rung to mark the passage of each half hour; thus, 3½ hours into the watch in question.

58 *pack up their traps*: here 'traps' refers to personal baggage, or cases for personal possessions.

  Haiphong: in modern Vietnam.

59 *half-a-crown*: a pre-decimalization British coin, silver in colour and earlier made from real silver, worth two shillings and sixpence, or one eighth of a pound sterling.

  sortilege: magical powers. The photograph described here has a close parallel in *Falk*.

61 *Pulo Condor*: now called Con Son; a group of 12 islands east of Cape Cambodia famous for a prison for political prisoners during the French occupation (information from Mr Seiji Minamida).

62 *He had made up his mind . . . everything*: note how much the ex-captain's state resembles that of the narrator at the start of the work.

  unknown powers that shape our destinies: another echo of *Hamlet*: see V. ii.

64 *tragic complexion*: at this point the following passage occurs in Conrad's manuscript (words in square brackets deleted in the manuscript): 'He was convinced that he was pleading for his life. I

on my side looked upon him as a [dead man already] a man finally
condemned, [with] and I [?with] suffered from the painful feeling
that if I [did what] followed ?in way of commonsense and true
compassion he would die execrating me as his murderer. To my
inexperience of life, responsible life, this seemed simply awful.
And also [criminally] atrociously unfair. For I was conscious of
nothing but the best intentions.'

65 *charter-party*: a legal document produced in duplicate, binding
the two parties receiving copies to its terms.

66 *Legation*: a diplomatic mission under a Minister (here represent-
ing Britain).

67 *choleraic symptoms*: Norman Sherry points out that a crew
member of the *Otago* did die of cholera, but before Conrad joined
the ship (*Conrad's Eastern World*, p. 230). The disease that affects
the rest of the crew, given their need for quinine, is clearly malaria.

68 *gharry*: a horse-drawn cart or carriage.

73 *inglorious fight*: in Conrad's manuscript this is followed by the
following passage, manuscript deletions in square brackets: 'It
was a deception. But ever since I [broke away] had broken away
?in discontent to find out something more about myself and about
life all the moments had been moments of deception. About
midday . . .'

mortal coil: another echo of *Hamlet*: III. i.

74 *anchor-watch*: an anchor-watch is a detachment of seamen kept
on deck for duties while a ship is at anchor.

75 *'What's the good . . . Mr Burns?'*: note that 'letting go [his] hold of
the ground only to drift' is, metaphorically, what the Captain had
done in leaving his previous ship. His question is indicative of
moral growth.

lonely responsibilities: a long passage follows at this point in
Conrad's manuscript which it is worth quoting in full (square
brackets are for Conrad's manuscript deletions):
'. . . lonely responsibility; weighed down, [by the solitude] by it
in that cabin, gloomy with the lamp turned down and where my
predecessor had expired under the eyes of a few awed seamen.
   The passage of death made of it like a vast solitude. I took
refuge from it in my state-room where [as I far as I knew nobody
had] nobody had died as far as I knew. After all the passion of
anger and indignation I had thrown into my activities on shore

the unpeopled stillness of that gulf weighed on my [me like an unpeopled] shaken confidence like a mere artifice of some [forthcoming ??] inimical force—I upbraided myself for [?that] the very existence of that unwholesome [sentiment] sensation [But] I resisted it. But [in] that [very ??] resistance [in] itself was a manifestation of a self-consciousness which was to me a strange [?to my] experience, distasteful and disquieting. I welcomed a great wave of fatigue that all at once overwhelmed me from head to foot [while] in I struggle[d] against morbidity.

Without taking off any of my clothing—not even removing my cap from my head I esconced myself in the corner of the couch and crossing my arms on my breast fell [profoun] into a profound slumber.

I dreamt of the Bull of Bashan. He was roaring beyond all reason on his side of a very high fence striking it with his forehoof and also rattling his [??horn] horns against it from time to time. On my side of the fence my purpose was (in my dream) to lead a contemplative existence. I despised the brute, but gradually a fear woke up in me—that he would end by breaking through— not through the fence—through my purpose. A horrible fear. I tried to ?fight [it ???] against it and mainly to keep it down with my hands. But it got the better of me like a [compressed] powerful compressed spring might have done—violently.

I found myself on my feet, very scared by my dream and in addition appalled by the apparition of the late captain in front of my open[?] door. For what else could be that dim [?featureless] figure in the [cuddy] half light of the cuddy, featureless, still malevolently silent, not to be mistaken for anything earthly.

Before my teeth began to rattle however the apparition spoke in a hoarse apologetic [?but flesh and blood] voice which no ghost would have [??] thought it necessary to adopt. Certainly not the ghost of that savage overbearing [man] sinner who [if he had been able] would have liked to take [?] his ship out of the world with him.

It was but the voice of the seaman on watch who had come down to tell me that there were faint airs off the land. Enough he thought to get underway with.

[?] I told him to call all hands to man the windlass. Before he left the cabin it occurred to me to ask him whether he had much trouble to wake me up.

"You were very sound off Sir" he said [?] with much feeling as he retired.'

EXPLANATORY NOTES 141

For the Bull of Bashan see particularly Psalm 22:12: 'Many bulls have compassed me: strong *bulls* of Bashan have beset me round.' The first verse of the psalm suggests, perhaps, an appropriateness to the captain's situation: 'My God, my God, why hast thou forsaken me? *Why art thou* so far from helping me, *and from* the words of my roaring?'

cuddy: a small cabin.

windlass: a mechanical contrivance for weighing the anchor.

yards: spars for supporting square sails.

76 *trucks*: the truck is a circular capping on the top of a mast.

77 *zenith*: highest point.

Cape Liant: in modern Thailand, outside Bangkok.

83 *bury our late captain right in the ship's way*: contrast a key element in Conrad's *The Nigger of the 'Narcissus'*, in which the curse hangs over the ship *until* the seaman Wait dies and is buried at sea.

I thought so: Conrad's manuscript has a typescript section here, which includes a long, crossed-out passage. Part of this I have quoted in my Introduction; another part gives an interesting statement of the neutrality of the elements: 'There was no reason for special apprehensions. The view presented an orderly perspective of [non] sea changes [on] and sea (results) familiar with the seaman's eye all over the world presenting no extraordinary images of evil or good. Upon the whole it was natural to my [ears] [eyes] age to see the universe mainly enveloped in sunshine and azure with something of the light enchantment in all its aspects, benign and [stern] severe.' (Square brackets include material deleted by Conrad before the final deletion; round brackets are Conrad's own.)

84 *Island of Koh-ring*: perhaps the island of Kho Rin in latitude 8°40′N. 106°30′E.

88 *braces*: long whips leading aft from the ends of the yard-arms by which the yards are swung at different angles with the keel while remaining horizontal.

malefices: wicked bewitchment.

92 *with their crews all dead*: the Flying Dutchman is mentioned specifically on page 94, but the situation also calls to mind that

depicted in Coleridge's 'The Rime of the Ancient Mariner'.

hirsute: hairy.

96 *quarter-deck*: a smaller deck, or part of the upper deck between the stern and the after-mast, often restricted to officers.

99 *all aback*: meaning that the sails are flat against the mast with the wind against their front.

cleat: pair of horns for making fast halliards, etc.

belaying pin: around which ropes would be coiled.

ringbolt: a bolt with an opening at one end which contains a ring.

100 *Gambril*: called Smith in Conrad's manuscript. A 'Gambril' also appears in *Falk*.

105 *binnacle*: a box near the helm in which the compass is kept.

106 *Mei-nam*: the Menam river, now known as Chao Phraya, which runs from the Burma–Laos border, crosses Thailand from north to south, and enters the Gulf of Siam through several outlets. (cf. the opening page of *The Secret Sharer*.)

109 *Titans*: in Greek mythology, the sons and daughters of Uranus (sky) and Gaea (earth), originally twelve in number. The myth includes their rising against—and castrating—their father and, eventually, being overcome and hurled into a cavity below Tartarus. Some of Conrad's descriptions here are very reminiscent of Keats's portrayals of the fallen Titans in his 'Hyperion'.

109 *leech-line*: the leech is the sloping or perpendicular side of a sail; a line is a rope used for trussing a sail.

114 *sleeping suit*: cf. *The Secret Sharer*, in which both the Captain and his double are clad at one point in sleeping suits.

115 *scuppers*: openings in ship's side to allow water to run away.

116 *lubber*: sailor's term for a clumsy seaman.

119 *brother . . .Brother . . .* : in Conrad's manuscript '. . . Brother to the devil.' (Conrad's ellipsis.)

125 *slat*: to flap.

126 *halliards*: rope or tackle for raising or lowering a spar.

get the anchors cock-billed: that is, with the anchors pointing downwards from the cat-head (a beam projecting almost horizontally from each side of the bows of the ship) ready to be dropped.

127 *bluejackets*: naval sailors as opposed to Merchant Marine sailors.

THE WORLD'S CLASSICS

A Select List

Youth, Heart of Darkness, The End of the Tether
Edited by Robert Kimbrough

DANIEL DEFOE: Moll Flanders
Edited by G. A. Starr

Robinson Crusoe
Edited by J. Donald Crowley

Roxana
Edited by Jane Jack

CHARLES DICKENS: David Copperfield
Edited by Nina Burgis

Dombey and Son
Edited by Alan Horsman

Little Dorrit
Edited by Harvey Peter Sucksmith

Martin Chuzzlewit
Edited by Margaret Cardwell

The Mystery of Edwin Drood
Edited by Margaret Cardwell

Oliver Twist
Edited by Kathleen Tillotson

Sikes and Nancy and Other Public Readings
Edited by Philip Collins

BENJAMIN DISRAELI: Coningsby
Edited by Sheila M. Smith

Sybil
Edited by Sheila M. Smith

FËDOR DOSTOEVSKY: Crime and Punishment
Translated by Jessie Coulson
With an introduction by John Jones

Memoirs from the House of the Dead
Translated by Jessie Coulson
Edited by Ronald Hingley

JOHN GALT: Annals of the Parish
Edited by James Kinsley

The Entail
Edited by Ian A. Gordon

The Provost
Edited by Ian A. Gordon

ELIZABETH GASKELL: Cousin Phillis and Other Tales
Edited by Angus Easson

Cranford
Edited by Elizabeth Porges Watson

Mary Barton
Edited by Edgar Wright

North and South
Edited by Angus Easson

Ruth
Edited by Alan Shelston

Sylvia's Lovers
Edited by Andrew Sanders

THOMAS HARDY: A Pair of Blue Eyes
Edited by Alan Manford

Jude the Obscure
Edited by Patricia Ingham

Under the Greenwood Tree
Edited by Simon Gatrell

The Well-Beloved
Edited by Tom Hetherington

The Eclogues and The Georgics
Translated by C. Day Lewis
Edited by R. O. A. M. Lyne

HORACE WALPOLE: The Castle of Otranto
Edited by W. S. Lewis

IZAAK WALTON and CHARLES COTTON:
The Compleat Angler
Edited by John Buxton
With an introduction by John Buchan